Steady Mobbin'

Marcellus Allen

Lock Down Publications and
Ca$h Presents
Steady Mobbin'
A Novel by Marcellus Allen

Marcellus Allen

Lock Down Publications
P.O. Box 870494
Mesquite, Tx 75187

Visit our website
www.lockdownpublications.com

Copyright 2018 by Steady Mobbin' Marcellus Allen

First Edition September 2018
Printed in the United States of America

Lock Down Publications
Like our page on Facebook: Lock Down Publications @
www.facebook.com/lockdownpublications.ldp
Cover design and layout by: **Dynasty Cover Me**
Book interior design by: **Shawn Walker**

4

Stay Connected with Us!

Text **LOCKDOWN** to 22828 to stay up-to-date with new releases, sneak peeks, contests and more…

Submission Guideline.

Submit the first three chapters of your completed manuscript to ldpsubmissions@gmail.com, subject line: Your book's title. The manuscript must be in a .doc file and sent as an attachment. The document should be in Times New Roman, double-spaced and in size 12 font. Also, provide your synopsis and full contact information. If sending multiple submissions, they must each be in a separate email.

Have a story but no way to send it electronically? You can still submit to LDP/Ca$h Presents. Send in the first three chapters, written or typed, of your completed manuscript to:

LDP: Submissions Dept
Po Box 870494
Mesquite, Tx 75187

DO NOT send original manuscript. Must be a duplicate.

Provide your synopsis and a cover letter containing your full contact information.

Thanks for considering LDP and Ca$h Presents.

Steady Mobbin'

ACKNOWLEDGEMENTS

Frist I gotta thank my Lord and Savior Jesus Christ! Through him all things are possible!

My MOM: For loving me unconditional no matter what and never leaving me. You truly are the best woman/mother in the world. I love you so much! Your faith keeps me going. POPS: For all the wisdom and sound advice.

JAQUES: Man lil' bro none of this would be possible without you! You do everything for me and then some. You believed in me from day one! I woulda been quit if it wasn't for you, Real Talk! I know I drive you crazy sometimes bro, forgive me. But we here now! We knew since 2015 I was gon' sign to "CASH" before he even knew! Now it's time to move to our next plans. Real estate and franchisement! Bro, I owe you so much, I got you!

SHAY: I love you best friend. You've always believed in me even when I was really thuggin it! You saw something in me I just recently saw in myself. Greatness! Without you I wouldn't be half the man I am and that's a fact.

LISA: I love you, sis. You've read, typed and helped me come up with so much of this story. You was the first person to read/love my book. Remember how mad you was at Cash and my editor for making me change so much? "They got you fucked up, bro." That was Epic. LOL Thank you.

GOTTI: You said yo girls didn't believe that was really you in the original book? Watch this! Antwan Anderson AKA Twan Gotti AKA Arrogant… Now they know! Love you, big bro for being a real nigga and never leaving me in here. Pushing my book and buying multiple copies. Giving me advice on the book and life.

PYREX: For the advice on my book and life and being my brother

ELIJAH/JAXX: For being my brother and a super real nigga! You aint never let me down.

RAMONE – EXIE – G'EARL: For being my brothers.

TYCKOON BOOYOW: No words necessary

LUMZ!: We till the casket.

Marcellus Allen

JOJO: My favorite relative! You know how much I love you. Hold ya head up, that murder beef almost over.

GEE: My Lincoln Park nigga! You my most loyal friend/nigga on this earth. Is there a realer nigga than you? Murda Gang!

MIKE: My Oaks Park nigga! F.A.B. 12TH Ave Blaaddaa! Yeah, I had to do that! You one of my only friends. I love you, bro! Thanks for staying up in the cell bouncing ideas for the book! You aint never switched up!

RESPECT: You a real nigga! Stay coming to visit me. It's Denver Lanes till the death of us.

BLEED: My main nigga! For Rockin since day 1 and keepin it Lanes. Most of 'em don't do it right.

LIL OSO: My lil' homey what's good? Lanes.

LIL DUTE: For talking with me about my book for hours and giving me ideas. Now finish yo book.

DONTAE CRAWFORD: My Mob piru 662 homie! You way too turn't up. I'm happy you won yo appeal and gave that 33 years back.

LIL FLASH- AKA TWIN: I put yo cry baby ass in the book! LOL You know I got love for you.

HOOCH: First homie to buy my original book!

NELLC: What'z good twin?

LAY G: My New Jersey Nigga.

SHOOTER: Love you nigga.

STIXX: Love you lil bro

LIL CHEWY: You my lil' nigga

GATMAN: You aint never changed one me!

GENO: My main nigga out there in Cali!

All my family! All the Anderson's.

All the real niggaz and women in prison. All my West Coast, down South, East Coast, Midwest, Damu homies. TAP in with me. Shout out to the real Kiwe's out there! To my two cities: Portland and L.A. To my niggaz on 109th Figueroa St. Yeah, I rep that! My Pasadena niggaz! I see you Big Cutthroat [Anthony Jolly] I know you want me and Bleed to switch over but I gotta keep it "Fig" when in L.A. It's all Lanes though!

8

Steady Mobbin'

TO MY GREAT LAWYERS: Ryan Scott and John Gutbezahl, y'all fight hard. My private investigator Cindy Borders for all you help, even helping me complete this book and get it to Cash.

To My Editor: Thankz for being so tough!

TO CASH: Thank you for signing me and putting your money behind me, for believing in my work. For helping me improve my writing. I owe you!

DEDICATION

To Darius "Lil Boobis" Perry and Davontae "Tae Ty" Kerney. I'm hurting without y'all. I talked to "Tae Ty" Jan 27, 2018 while writing this book. He was dead two days later, I still cry.

R.I.P. LIST

Marcellus Allen Sr., Dickie Anderson Jr., Lil Boobis, Tae Ty, Lil 8, Stixx, Turk, Dar, Ghost, Dragon, Smash, Carl, Tripp, Overdose, CAM, Black Sean, Loco Will, … They killed my niggaz! My mom asked me when will we stop killin' each other? I told her I don't know… Think on that.

Steady Mobbin'

My Wife,

I don't know who you are but I can't wait to meet you. Sign here if that's you. _____x

My Info: Marcellus Allen – 15954768
777 Stanton Blvd
Ontario, Oregon 97914

Facebook: "Marcellus The Writer"
Instagram: "Marcellus The Writer"

Marcellus Allen

Steady Mobbin'

Chapter 1
May 1st, 2017

Slurp! Slurp! Slurp! Tamia was giving me that fire dome while I was sitting on her couch watching her head bob up and down.

"Ahh, shit I'm 'bout to bust!" I moaned out, then gripped the sides of her head.

I started face fucking her, really trying to get my rocks off. When I felt myself getting ready to blast off, I jumped off the couch and sped the pace up. She was on her knees taking the dick like a champ. She gripped my hips for leverage and got to bopping her neck even faster trying to keep up with my pace.

Slurp! Slurp! We had the room sounding like a dick sucking porno. That was the main reason I stayed coming over here, Tamia had the best head in Portland!

"Agghh! Here it come, you ready?" I yelled.

She just nodded her head, while keeping eye contact with me. I don't know what it was about that shit, but I loved it!

"Agghh! Shit! Ahh!" I roared, after finally busting in her mouth.

I stood there looking down at her, while she swallowed every drop like a real bitch, then leaned my head back in ecstasy as she slowly took it out her mouth.

"All done, papi," she said in her sexy ass Latin accent that she really brought to life whenever we were getting it in, she knew I loved that shit.

Tamia was one of those black Dominican bitches. The ones that's dark skinned, but speak that Spanish shit fluent. Her mom looked like a regular Spanish chick with no black in her, but her dad was jet black and they both came from that Island together. The best way to describe her is to think about that chick "Juju" from Love and Hip Hop. Chocolate skin tone, long hair, fat ass, but Spanish speaking.

"Damn, baby, you the best," I complimented her.

"I know, now sit down, 'cause you ain't going nowhere till after I get some dick," she told me, then stood up and pushed me down on the couch. "I'm 'bout to go turn my Bryson Tiller on, don't move," she said, then walked off ass hole naked.

I was watching that ass jiggle with each step that she took through the den, until she rounded the corner into the living room. My dick got back rock hard from the thoughts that were running through my mind, until I heard Jhene Aiko start singing from my cell phone.

I pulled my pants up and grabbed my phone from my pocket, then looked at the caller I.D even though only one person had that ringtone. "The Wife" was blasted across the screen. I was debated if I should answer it or not, then I heard Bryson Tiller come through the speaker and that decided that dilemma right there.

The lights got dim, now I knew she was in the kitchen, because that's where all the switches are located. Then she appeared at the entrance and started doing these sexy poses for me. I also noticed how she had put on some six-inch red heels.

Oh, she's going all out for a real nigga tonight. That was my last thought before the door got kicked in. Tamia screamed and tried to run towards me, but fell flat on her face, then I went to work. I snatched my .45 off the table at the same time that two niggas rocking blue bandanas on their faces came rushing in, guns drawn.

Boom! Boom! Boom! Boom! Boom!

I let loose on them crabs without any hesitation. I knew they weren't there to talk it out. They backed into the kitchen and then fired shots from around the doorway.

Boca! Boca! Boca! Boca

All I could see were their arms stretched out towards me, shooting at whatever. They weren't even aiming, just shooting. I must have surprised them and threw them off their game plan. I watched Tamia get up and run into the bathroom.

I took off down the hallway, headed to her room, so I could get the fuck out.

Boca! Boca! Boca!

Them pussies started shooting at my back.

Steady Mobbin'

Boom Boom! Boom! I returned fire over my shoulder at them. To keep it real, I wasn't even aiming, I just needed some separation.

I made it to her room and locked the door as soon as I stepped foot in that bitch. *Take a deep breath, I know what I'm doing.* I don't know why those Meek Mill lyrics from *Toy Story 3* always popped into my head every time I was in a critical situation and had to breathe.

I broke over to the window that led to the parking lot and opened it like my life depended on it.

"Open up bitch ass slob!" One of the gunmen taunted me.

"Come get me!" I yelled back.

Boom! Boom! Boom!

I sent some hot shit through the door, then jumped out the window. In the movies, niggas hid in the room and killed the ones behind the door, but not in real life, so I didn't try that shit.

I sprinted through the lot, headed straight for my all white 750 Beamer, but for some reason I couldn't remember exactly where I parked it. I think it was because I entered the lot from a different angle coming from the window.

Boca! Boca! Boca!

"Scary ass nigga!" One of them yelled out the window.

I was about to bust back, but I spotted my ride and decided I'd catch up with them in the near future.

"Siri, call Bobbie," I spoke to my iPhone as soon as I peeled out the lot.

I connected my Bluetooth, while I waited for that nigga to answer. I couldn't believe niggas had the heart to try me like that, especially in the Ville! I wondered how the fuck did they know I was in there? And more important, how did they know to come in there right when the lights went out! That made me think of Tamia.

"What's brackin?" Bobbie's deep raspy voice came blasting through the car interrupting my train of thought.

"Somebody just kicked Tamia's door down and tried to end me! Have everybody meet at my spot right now!"

"Nigga, what? We ridin' tonight!" he yelled back.

"Naw, come to my spot first," I demanded, then disconnected the call.

***

One hour later

We were all posted up in my basement, in the living room, having a meeting. I had one of those basements that shouldn't even be called a basement, it was more like a lounge. It had a mini kitchen, with a bar, a pool table, a living room and I even had a studio down there. This was where all our meetings were held.

Only my top dogs were allowed at the air, I kept my inner circle small, in hopes that I could never get snitched on or betrayed.

Every person in that room was considered my brother. With that exception for Jersey Joe, I had grown up with each one since middle school.

Bobbie was my right-hand man. I didn't make a move without him. I trusted that nigga with my life, period. He was one of those niggas that didn't want nothing out of life but to be a gangsta. He still wore Dickies and rocked the red Chucks with 'em sometimes. Dark skinned, short, sneaky and one hundred percent loyal, was the best way to describe him.

"So, what's up blood, you think Tamia set you up?" Bobbie asked.

That was a good question, that I had asked myself a hundred times before I even got inside my house. I kept going back to the look on her face when we heard the door getting kicked down.

"Naw, I don't think so, she good," I answered, after picturing her face one more time.

"She guilty, blood, how else they know when to come in? Why she ain't dead? Think about it. Let me go kill her, set an example real quick," Burnside spoke up.

Steady Mobbin'

That was his usual response to everything. The best way to describe him was he was quick to kill, flashy and flamboyant, and just didn't give a fuck. He would kill in broad daylight, without thinking twice.

"You think everybody guilty, nigga, calm down. I already told you why she ain't dead, she hid in the bathroom, then ran out when they started shooting at me inside her room. She Gucci, bro."

"Yo, son, if we ain't gone kill her then who we gone kill? Somebody gotta die, son, word is bond," Jersey Joe added his two cents.

I already knew he was about to do Burnsides ad-libs, I was just waiting on him. Joe and Burnside are first cousins and are exactly alike. Actually, Joe was worse than Burnside, he was a straight live wire. He was from New Jersey, but he had been n Portland for a few years now.

"C'mon, nigga, you know we killing somebody about this. That ain't even a question. We just gotta figure out which one of those crabs actually had the audacity to try me," I responded.

"Now we know," Gotti finally said something. He completed the circle and as usual, he was the last one to speak. He was my real family, our mothers are sisters, but we are more like brothers. We were raised in the same house, so we had that strong bond. He was a few years older, so I considered him my big bro'. He was about his money above anything else, but he would catch a body if he needed to.

"Know what?" I asked him.

"Who tried to get at you, look," he said, then held his phone out, so we could all see it. "One of my bitches just sent me this screenshot."

I got to burning up inside as I read each word. Yeah, I made up my mind at that moment that I was killing all those niggas! Some lil' nigga named Pull-Out made a post saying, "It's crazy when you see the so-called king of the town running for his life. The squad out tonight."

I looked at Bobbie and saw he was feeling the same way that I was. Yeah, I knew exactly who was behind this now. The Gutta Squad niggas. The lil' nigga, Pull-Out was Butta's lil' brother, and Butta was their leader. About time these niggas grew some balls and got back at us.

We'd been feuding with those crabs since high school, but over the last year it's been heating up. To make a long story short, Burnside was fucking this nigga named Half-Dead's baby mama and the shit hit the fan in the club. Half-Dead caught the two in the club and flexed on Burnside and we ended up beating the shit out of him and clapping on his homies.

"I'm killing them niggas tonight, blood," Burnside spat, with anger in his voice.

"Word is bond," Joe just had to say.

"Naw, its Gucci, go home and get some pussy," I replied.

"Nigga, what? Fuck that, we riding tonight. Bitch ass niggas shooting shots at us on Facebook, we riding tonight. They gotta know we coming for them," Burnside argued with me.

"You know what?" I started to explain myself, then dialed a number on my phone and put it on speaker.

"Who dis?" a voice answered the phone.

"The mob himself, you fat ass, bitch ass, niggas. Yo' brother lil' post just sealed ya casket bitch," I told Butta's bitch ass.

He started laughing, then said, "I heard you're a track star now, stop calling my phone, slob ass nigga."

"My nigga, Burnside, wants you to know that we're on you, tell ya mama to get those flowers ready," I threatened him, then hung up on his punk ass.

"He knows now, nigga," I told Burnside, then stood up stretching.

"Yea, that's a good idea cause I'm tired as fuck and its past one o'clock, Trina bout to be trippin," Gotti said, then got off the couch, ready to go home.

"Everybody just chill for the night, Burnside, slide through in the morning I got something important to talk to you about,"

Steady Mobbin'

I said, then headed to my room so I could pass out. It had been a long day, but the shit was just getting started.

Marcellus Allen

Chapter 2
May 2nd, 2017

"Marshawn! Marshawn! Wake up, nigga, I know you hear me! Wake up!" Olay yelled at me, while shaking my shoulders.

I was playing sleep, I had been up the last forty-five minutes, the moment she started getting dressed. I knew what was coming but I was hoping to delay it at least until later that night.

"Why are you pushing me and yelling this early in the morning? You gon' wake Mar-Mar up, what time is it? Damn!" I said, faking an attitude. I grabbed my I-phone to check the time, "It's eight thirty-five in the morning, what do you want?" I asked, still playing dumb and half sleep.

She folded her arms, then responded, "Why you ain't tell me you got shot at last night? You came in here last night like everything was normal, I knew something wasn't right, having a meeting at midnight and shit. Since when do we keep secrets from each other?"

I finally sat   up, it was time to face the situation and get it over with. The look of concern that was on her face made me feel guilty for even putting her through this. I stared at wifey for a few seconds, just taking her all in.

She had on a red Nike golf shirt, beige khakis, and a red Nike snap back. She had her hair in a long ponytail, looking like a professional golfer. Olay is 5'6, light skinned, hair down to her shoulders, with a petite body frame. Even when she was rocking her golf attire, her natural beauty couldn't be ignored. To keep it real, Olay was my everything. I loved her with my whole heart for numerous reasons. We first met at church, when we were twelve years old and we've been rocking since. We've always had some type of relationship while growing up, either close friends or fucking around. I trusted her completely with everything I was worth.

"What are you staring at? Are you going to answer my question or what?" Her voice broke my concentration.

Marcellus Allen

"I was just sitting here thinking about how beautiful you are. Like seriously, you're a work of art. I'm surprised nobody pain'ted a portrait of you yet. Then, when you get mad and stare with your arms crossed, its priceless. Come here, baby, come talk to daddy," I told her, trying to break her wall down.

She kept that face of stone, but I knew deep down inside she was melting away. She knows she can't stay mad at me, I know all of her weak spots.

"Nigga, I done heard it all before in the last what? Eleven, twelve, thirteen years? But what I ain't heard, is an answer to my question! You sitting here procrastinating, cause you know you're in the wrong. Nigga, what was you doing at that bitch Tamia's house in the first place?" she yelled at me, really mad.

I was trying to think of the right words to say when my son came crashing into the room. His lil' bad ass did his usual entrance, pushed open the door, making it slam against the wall, then stood there staring at us as if he challenged us to say something.

"Boy, what yo' bad ass want?" Yo' mama woke you up, huh?" I said to him.

"I'm hungry, daddy," he whined, then came over to get picked up for me to pick him up. I kissed him on the forehead, then put him back down.

"Go wait at the table for mommy, she'll be right there," I told him.

"C'mon, mommy!" he told her excitedly, before he ran out of the room.

That was little Marshawn, but we call him Mar-Mar and the lil nigga looked and acted just like me, I mean the nigga was a spitting image of me already and he was only two years old. I walked over to the mirror and started brushing my waves. I could see Olay still standing behind me with her hands on her hips. I looked at myself from head to toe, since she was staring so hard.

I stood 6'1 and weighed about 170 pounds. I'm carmel skin toned, rocked Dolce & Gabbana prescription glasses, oh and did

Steady Mobbin'

I mention I had waves that were dipping out of control? I'ma straight fly nigga and I only rock that designer shit.

"So, are you gone stand there and not answer my question? Why were you at that bitch house?" she asked again.

"So, if I woulda got shot at in the Lloyd center or in my car then it wouldn't be an issue, right? You're not concerned about if I'm okay or not, you just wanna know about the bitch, right? You waking me up in the morning over some bitch? Shit, at least cook a nigga some breakfast or give a nigga some head or summthin got damn!" I said, trying to make her feel guilty.

When I turned around she still had the same look on her face, I guess my plan wasn't working. I exhaled loudly to show my frustration, then sat down on the edge of the bed.

"It's an organization called the D.E.A. you've heard of them, right? Anyway, their only goal in life is to lock up drug dealers. Now, unless you forgot how you got those diamonds and all your clothes, let me remind you, I'ma drug dealer. I sell drugs!" I yelled that last part out, causing her to jump then I continued, "Rule number one, never leave drugs and money where you sleep at. So, that means I can't leave 'em here or we're both going to jail. So, us smart drug dealers use people's houses that we really don't care about, usually a bitch.

Tamia's spot is one of the few that I use. I pay her rent, furnish the spot and whatever else. She holds my dope, money, guns and whatever else I need her to. So, to answer yo' question I was going to pick up some dope. Then some crabs kicked down the door and we had a shootout. That's the story!" I gave her most of the truth except Tamia wasn't just any bitch to me, but I couldn't tell her that.

"Whatever, nigga, I know one thing, ain't no bitch gone put her life on the line unless she loves the nigga. So, are you fucking her, nigga?" she asked, then stared right through me waiting for my response.

My phone started ringing before I could lie to her because I damn sho' wasn't about to tell the truth. I knew by the ringtone that it was my big brother, Jaxx, calling.

"What's mobbing, big bro? This early? A'ight, I'm on the way," I told him, then left the room without saying a word to Olay, but I could feel her stare burning on the back of my neck.

Twenty minutes later I pulled up at my brother's place. Jaxx opened the door before I could even knock. That meant he'd been standing there waiting on me, which also meant he was about to lecture me. He looked me up and down twice, then shook his head before saying, "I see you're still alive and in one piece."

"This is me, is that you?" I shot, spitting that Portland slang, which meant *yeah, nigga, I'm alive, is you stupid*, and then I walked into the house.

I don't know why I had to say that shit, especially since I knew he was about to lecture me about that weak ass shooting. I loved my big brother to death, but he is a straight hypocrite, on me. He was always talking that peaceful shit, but he was one of the biggest drug dealers in the state.

He thought   since he wasn't a gang member and out riding on niggas that he wasn't a part of the problem. The funny thing is, he was my connect. Bro sat on the couch and let his dreads out of the ponytail that they were in. *Aww shit, the nigga done got comfortable*, I thought.

"Look, brah, I just got done getting lectured by Olay and I got hella shit to do today so can we get to the money or what?" I said, hoping he would spare me the speech.

"Your life is worth more than money, lil' nigga. Why I gotta hear about you almost dying from the streets instead of from you?" he asked

I sucked my teeth, then said, "I wasn't even close to dying, them fools was barely aiming. And man, I'm not about to be calling you every time I fall off my bike like I'm some bitch ass nigga or something, don't trip, Bro, I got this," I said, then opened up the bag I had brought with me. I was hoping that when he seen all those dead presidents staring at him he would shut the fuck up.

Steady Mobbin'

"Here go yo' money," I added for extra effect.

"I told you yo' life is worth more than money, now what you gone do?" he asked. Bro just couldn't let it go.

"Fuck them lames, blood, they won't make it to see Christmas, and that's only 'cause I feel like being nice."

"You really think this shit is a joke, huh? You think your untouchable? I've seen the untouchable get touched way too many times in my life." He tossed a duffel bag to me.

I caught it, and then I looked inside just for the hell of it. Ten bricks were looking at me, just begging me to add baking soda on 'em. That's what the fuck I was talking about. "You need a massage, or something to take yo' mind off the bullshit. You and the rest of the town already know I'ma kill them niggas without even breaking a sweat," I said, then made my way to the door.

"You needa start takin yo' music career more serious and leave these streets alone," he advised me.

"You sound like Spike now," I shot back

Looking back at it now, I was the hottest rapper in the town. Everybody kept saying how I was the next to blow, especially Spike. I wasn't focused on no rap deal, what the fuck could a label offer me?

I finally made my way out with the dope and seen Bobbie and Tamia talking about nothing, leaning up against her car. The sun was out, and it was hot as a muthafucka, but I was about to heat things up. I threw the bag to Bobbie, then hopped in my car without saying a word. There was no need to, we'd been through this a hundred times, plus I was irritated as fuck. Tamia jumped in the passenger seat and I took off without acknowledging her either.

"Uh, hi to you, too." She decided to speak, after staring at me for a few blocks.

I looked at her for a split second, then focused back on the road. I didn't feel like talking and I was still going over the whole shooting in my head. The look on her face before the shooting was the only reason why she was still alive. Just thinking about it made me get all hot inside, I felt like killing a nigga that night.

I had to remind myself to stick to the plan, I had something real nice for the Gutta Squad bitches.

"Nigga, I know you ain't siting there with an attitude like a bitch did something wrong to you," she told me with a voice full of attitude.

"Tamia, how did they know I was in yo' spot? And tell me why they kicked the door down right after the lights went out?" I said to her, real calm.

"What the fuck is you trying to insinuate? You got me highly fucked up," she yelled at me, then gave me a look that could kill.

"I'm not insinuating anything, I'm just curious about a few things."

"Fuck you! After everything I've done for you over these past years! Now you wanna sit here and accuse me of setting you up, fuck you!" She turnt up on me, then like any other woman would, she started to cry. "What would I gain from that, Marshawn? Huh? Getting the only man that I love killed, for what? I've been nothing but loyal to you, nigga, since day one. I let you get away with murder, muthafucka! I'm loyal and faithful to you even though you go home to that golf playing bitch every night! Fuck you, I'm done with you," she continued to yell, while crying at the same time.

I was dead wrong, and I knew it, even back then. Most of the time I did and said shit just to get a reaction out of people. I did want to see how she would respond, but on some real shit, I went too far. Even though I sometimes acted like Tamia was just some side bitch to me, she wasn't. When I first knocked her back in 2013 that's all she was, but over the years I ended up loving her.

She did everything a nigga asked of her and more. She was a thorough bitch all the way across the board. The only reason I didn't wife her up was because I already had a real queen. I was never going to leave Olay, she was my world. But at times, it did feel like Tamia was the better choice. Olay never gave me a reason to cheat on her like I always did, it was just the dog in me.

Steady Mobbin'

"And another thing, nigga, if I wanted to set you up I would of did it much better. I would of took all your money and dope and had somebody kill you in your sleep and left Portland for good! Punk ass, nigga." She added fuel to the fire.

Soon as that *punk* word left her mouth, I knew it was time to turn her down. In any other circumstance that would have gotten her slapped, but I told myself I had earned that one.

"I didn't think you set me up, baby, I was just fucking with you, my bad. You know if I really thought you did that you would've been dead." That was my way of apologizing and proving to her that I wasn't serious.

"Umm, I can't tell. Niggas sho' is bragging on Facebook about it," she shot back, trying to get under my skin.

I didn't even entertain her little mind games, I knew how to really get under her skin. I turned Kevin Gates CD all the way up and bobbed my head to 'em, totally ignoring her until we had got to the Condos.

Hours Later/The Studio

After I copped Tamia that new condo downtown, then dicked her down, she was back to normal. Once that was out the way, I headed straight to the recording studio where all my dawgs were. Them fools had it poppin' before I even got there. But when I did make my entrance it was all eyes on me, the usual.

It was about fifteen bitches in there and only ten of my homies. That was my type of atmosphere, right there. There were guns laying everywhere, from the couches to the tables and even a few big ones leaned up against the wall.   Pills were on the tables by the bulk and powder was everywhere by the line. Bitches were twerking' and niggas was smokin', yeah, it was live!

"What's brackin', blood? I'm ready to kill one of them niggas," Bobbie said in his raspy ass voice, then passed me the blunt he was smoking.

27

Marcellus Allen

"They won't make it through the summer," I replied, then hit the blunt a few times after I found a spot on the couch.

"All this pussy in here and you thinking about some niggas," I added, then burst out laughing and coughing at the same time.

"Blood, I can't even get on nothin' cause Falon in here hating and shit. She actin' like we in a real relationship or something," he complained.

"Here she come right now, too, stop complaining, you know you like the shit." I hit the blunt again while I watched Falon walk over to us.

Falon was Olay's little sister, but they acted nothing alike. They even had completely different body types. Falon was a straight amazon and one of the thickest bitches I'd ever seen. She needed to be on the cover of a   magazine, real talk. She was a bad bitch and she knew it, that's why any nigga that wanted to talk to her had to pay. She was a gold digger and didn't hesitate to let anybody know it. I had love for Falon though, she was like my lil' sis. Bobbie was a straight trick, perfect match.

"What's good, big bro, you ready to ride on those niggas or what? Just give me the plan," she said to me, while taking a seat on Bobbie's lap.

"Falon, shut yo' ass up cause you ain't gon' do shit but cry when shit hits the fan," I responded.

"What, nigga? I got bodies!"

"Yeah, on that pussy!" I shot back.

She punched me in the chest. "You got me fucked up, nigga!"

"Yo, O, you ready or what?" Ruger yelled at me from across the room before I could respond to Falon.

"Yeah, start that shit up!" I answered him.

Ruger was my in-house engineer, producer, and whatever else I needed him to be. He also was the one that leased the building for the studio, well at least on paper.

"Drop that *War Pain* for me, I got somethin' for them niggas, we bout to heat the summer up," I told him, then stepped into the booth.

Steady Mobbin'

I looked out the window and everybody was staring at me, they knew they were about to witness history being made. I can still feel that feeling just by thinking back on it. That was the shit that I lived for, the show, the power, to high sight on a muthafucka, which meant stunnin'.

Spike walked into the room and I got even more juiced up. "Hit the lights, blood," I spoke in the mic and they immediately went out.

Then I pulled my red flag out and hung it over the microphone like I always did. I threw up the 'B' and then threw up the Mob at the crowd then they all threw it back at me. Then I did what I always did last, I took my shirt off and tossed it on the ground. I looked at my .45 sticking out my waist and that was all I needed to complete the show, I was ready. Ruger dropped the instrumental right on time,

"Location/ Northeast Portland/ Mob headquarters studio to be exact/ Mood/ I just copped ten bricks from the play this morning, then went and bought my side bitch a condo downtown, how you think I feel/ Status/ Bullets don't tough me, them chumps gone be dead before Halloween/ ha ha/" I said into the mic, copying Meek Mills intro, but with my own lil' twist.

That's when I looked at everybody, looking at me. Nobody knew I was planning on dropping a diss track, I had everybody's attention.

"So, they sent some fuck boys, told em come and clap me/ I'm ten bricks up still smiling cause I'm trigga happy/ Niggas start to shoot and don't think to aim/ you just dug yo' grave, welcome to the hunger games/ see a Gutta Squad chain have Burnside take that shit/ I'ma have em sitting around like I hate that bitch/ Half Dead's baby mama I should break that bitch/ but Burnside just fucked her, then you ate that bitch/ I'ma send Bobbie with the mask to ya pad/ Tell 'em tie ya mama up while Joe search for the cash/ Burnsides body coming soon we just waiting/ when ya count a million with ya hands it's way to have patience/ lights went out I got to shootin' gotta kill me if I'm losing/ they hid in the kitchen oh this beef gone be a doozy/ if ya paid for the hit I hope ya kept a receipt/ to pay for ya casket, you fat bitch, you gone die in this beef."

I took my headphones off and picked up my shirt while everybody was yelling and cheering. A few of my niggas was over-exaggerating, falling on the ground and shit. I can't lie, I loved that shit. If only we would have known how much that song was going to get us in trouble. If only everybody knew how prophetic that verse was. I did cause I planned that shit. That was one of the dumbest moves of my life, but it felt good at the time.

Everybody bombarded me as soon as I stepped out the booth. All I heard was: *that shit was hard. Fuck those niggas. When did you write that?* I just shook everybody up and soaked up the praise.

"Yo, Bobbie!" I yelled out to him, after I spotted him still sitting on the couch with Falon. "Is you gon' be my Omelly or what? It's still an open verse on there!" I told him.

"Nigga, you better kill that shit, blood!" Burnside yelled out, egging him on.

"Yo son, make sure you say the east coast grim reaper name, too!" Jersey Joe added.

Bobbie hopped up like we hadn't said nothing and diddy bopped his way towards the booth.

"Aye, nigga? Make sure you talk that slick shit that Omelly was talkin' before the verse. All the triple OG shit," I said, as he walked by.

"Blood, this is what I do," he responded in his usual cocky manner.

"Let me holla at you in the office," Spike said, then walked off.

I was hoping that nigga wasn't on no lecturing bullshit, 'cause I'd had enough of that the last few days. When we got inside my office he leaned against my desk and was wearing one those lecture faces, that's when I knew it was coming.

Spike was from the hood that I grew up in, Unthank Park aka Portland Denver lanes. He used to put that work in, but then he got on some music shit. He moved to Atlanta and changed his name to Non-Stop after he started making beats. We heard his career really took off, when he made the beat for Yo Gotti's hit single 'Everybody.' Ever since then he'd been riding me hard about my music shit!

"So, what's the move? What we doin'?" he asked.

"What you mean?" I asked, even though I knew exactly what he was talking about.

"You know what I mean, nigga, yo music. You, Mozzy and Filthy Rich are the hottest niggas in the West Coast underground right now, but you playing. You know the only difference between you and them? They actually travel and do shows, actually network."

"I told you I'm 'bout to get on it, I just gotta make a few more moves. I can't just up and leave, I got money out here in these streets," I replied, then grabbed the duffel bag out the closet and dumped the bricks that I copped earlier on the desk. "This shit is real with me, blood and you know that," I added, while pounding my fist on my chest.

"You being a lil' too literal in yo' music, lil' bro, slow that shit down," he told me, then gave me a look of disappointment. "I know a lot of niggas in the pen right now for saying the wrong shit in their music," he gave me some game.

I waved my arm at him, dismissing what he said. "They gone have to bring in the national guard when they come get me, blood."

"A'ight, I hear you, Scarface. Anyway, I got an early flight in the morning, so I'm 'bout to head to the telly. Think about what I said and remember that time waits for no man." He gave me a 'G' hug.

"I'll be ready by the winter to move with this music shit. Right now, I got niggas to kill in the summer."

Marcellus Allen

Steady Mobbin'

Chapter 3
May 2nd – Same Night

I stayed in the room for like an hour by myself thinking about my life and where I was headed. I didn't understand why Spike wanted me to choose between music and the streets. Shit, I always thought they went hand in hand. Don't get me wrong I knew most of those rap niggas was frontin', rappin' their big brother's life and shit. But there were still a handful of those niggas that were still in the streets.

I'm not going to lie, I definitely wanted to live that rapper lifestyle, but shit, I was damn near doing that. This street shit was embedded in me though, it was part of my DNA. I loved getting money, I loved to shoot bitch niggas in their big ass mouths. I loved the power, and above everything else, I loved to be seen. There wasn't a better high in the world than to put on a show. I told myself *fuck that, I'ma have the best of both worlds.*

I walked out to the main room and it was still poppin like it was when I left. I noticed Jersey Joe sitting on the couch next to Falon, looking all in love and shit. It looked like he was trying to spit game on the low, but I discarded that though, 'cause Bobbie was still in the building. Technically, they all were single, but pussy was known to bring down empires.

I thought about walking over there and seeing what was really up, but then decided against it, 'cause I knew Joe knew better than that.

"We put that song on the net about thirty minutes ago and it's already everywhere. All the niggas are fuckin' with it and the bitches are loving it!" Gotti told me, while shoving his phone in my face.

I looked at all the post and comments on Facebook then gave it back, "Tell the circle to clear this shot out then all come to the back, I got that work for y'all." I took one last look at Joe and Falon before walking back to the office.

"Aight, everybody gone, blood, now where the money at?" Burnside asked, as he and the rest of the crew burst through the door, ten minutes later.

I didn't even feel the need to respond to the nigga since the work was right there on the table. They all looked at it, then took their seats.

"So, do we know who ran in the spot on me?" I asked the group.

"Pull-Out and his weak ass right hand man, Ron. He calls himself Ron the Don," Gotti answered.

"And I guess we already know the why?!" I looked at Burnside.

"That situation, plus they want us out of the way, so they can control all the dope," Gotti responded.

"This drama between us been goin' on for too long, it's time to end it. I just hope this shit don't take forever," I vented.

'Fuck them crabs, son, let's get all them niggas out the way right now. Apply pressure and knock the heads off. The rest of the crabs gone jump back in barrel where they belong, word is bond," Joe spoke up, ready for war.

"O, if we don't get right back, then half the town gone be gunnin' for our spot thinkin' we went soft," Bobbie said.

"I want Butta, Pressha, Dirty Dan, Pull-Out, Ron, Half-Dead and Gucci Ty, all dead by the end of summer. That's their head, second in command and their future. I don't ever want them niggas to resurface. And how the fuck did they get into 'The Ville' when that's supposed to be our stronghold?" I felt myself getting mad.

"That's a good question," Bobbie stated in a matter of fact tone.

"Y'all niggas fix that first! That can never happen again. Somethin' tells me I was set up," I replied, then walked out the room.

***

May 3rd/ Next Day

Steady Mobbin'

I was driving through the town on my dolo trip, getting to the money. My nigga, Mike, hit me up talking 'bout he wanted half a brick hard, so I was on the way. I damn near didn't leave the house though, 'cause it was raining, but like typical Portland weather, it got hot ten minutes after the rain stopped.

My phone went off and it showed somebody calling from O.S.P., Oregon State Penitentiary. I loved when my niggas called from the pen, that shit made my day. I received three to four calls a day from my niggas all throughout the state. I kept money on my phone account and had Tamia put bread on all my niggas books every first of the month. I listened to the stupid ass operator, then pressed five when I heard my relative, J-Mafia, say his name.

"What's mobbing, nigga?" I answered.

"Shit, you tell me, family, I heard it's *triv* out there," he responded.

It always amazed me how niggas in jail always got the news so fast. "Just a lil' misunderstanding, but you know the situation gone get adjusted," I replied.

"They got a few homies in here. Gee wanna get on em ASAP. I told him and the rest of those Lincoln Park niggas to wait till I called you, so what's up?"

I thought hard about it and decided to let them niggas breathe easy. I liked for my niggas to do their time as easy as possible. Most of the bros were doing football numbers and needed to stay in the visiting room, not the hole.

"Naw, relative, y'all just fall back. If I need to set an example then I'll let y'all know." I said.

"You sure?"

"Yeah, and tell that nigga Bleed to get all his rest while he can cause when he gets out next month it's gone be all work," I said.

"He already ready," he replied, then laughed.

"Aight, I gotta get this money real quick and I'm federal right now. Tap in with me tomorrow," I told him, then ended our call as I pulled up next to Mike.

We were parked a few houses down from my grandfather old house on 23rd and Killingsworth St. We were in the Piru hood, but I was good over there. Mike hopped out of his car and jumped in mine as soon as I pulled up.

"What's brackin?" he greeted me, then dropped a brown paper bag in my lap.

I reached under the seat and grabbed the work, then dropped it on him. "Shit, just mobbing. This the same work from last time."

"This the same money from last time," he replied, then laughed at his own joke.

"Aight, hit me when its heavy, blood," I said, then shook him up.

"Already," he replied then jumped out the whip.

I sped off, headed to my lunch date with Olay at the Olive Garden. I looked at my Rolex to see how late I was running. I was ten minutes late. I knew I would be   a lil' late if I decided to go get that money, but shit, she would just have to understand. Right when I was about to call her, I saw a nigga named Mike coming out the liquor store that I knew was a straight bitch.

My heart   pounded as I tried to figure out how I should handle the situation. I wanted to just air the niggas out, but at the same time I felt like he wasn't worth the bullets. I wanted to kill the main niggas, not a peon.

Mike wasn't shit but a Gutta Squad groupie . He posed in pictures with those niggas looking all tough and shit. Got a lil' money with them, but overall, he was all talk, high power on social media. Once I figured out how I was going to play it, I smirked to myself.

I watched him jump in his Lexus, then head towards the only exit out of the lot. That was the death trap of that place and why I never went to J's market. I pulled into the lot right when I thought he was leaving, and positioned myself where I was blocking him off.

I jumped out immediately with my gun aimed right at his face, as I speed-walked to him. Our eyes locked in on each other and that's when I saw all the bitch come out of him. He mouthed *aww shit* to himself and he was right. I yanked open the door and put the burner right to his head.

"Give me one reason why I shouldn't blow yo' face off, bitch ass nigga!" I growled.

"Man, I ain't got nothing to do with what happened to you. That's on my dead mama," he whined.

"Nigga, fuck yo' dead mama! You like talking shit on Facebook, right? This what we going to do, "I said, then pulled my I-phone out. I turned on the camera, then looked around real quick to make sure nobody was coming or calling the police. "Take them Jordan's off and that fake ass watch. Hurry up before I get mad!" I barked.

"Psshh, damn, cuz," he whined, then started taking his shit off.

"Nigga, fuck crabs! Drop that shit on the ground and hurry up. Matter of fact, say fuck crabs right now," I demanded

He leaned over and tossed the items on the ground then mumbled, "Fuck crabs."

"S ay it louder like you mean it, bitch ass nigga!" I yelled, then adjusted my aim.

" Fuck crabs!"

"Now get yo' bitch ass outta here and tell the rest of those crabs I'm out here!"

He sped off like a NASCAR driver the second I closed the door. I aimed my phone at his car fleeing the scene. When the Lexus was no longer visible, I picked his shit up and jumped in my car. But before I took off, I put my heat on the floor then aimed the camera at my face.

"My name is O dog from mob life and I approve this message," I said, then left.

Marcellus Allen

I pulled up to the Olive Garden thirty minutes late and I could tell by the look on Olay's face that she was hot. I tried to kiss her on the lips and she turned her face on me.

"Don't come in here late as hell and try to kiss me like we cool or something," she said as I sat down. "Yeah, you are taking me shopping and I know exactly what new bag I want. So, what held you up longer, picking up money or takin that niggas shoes on Instagram?" she asked, then slanted her eyes at me.

Damn! I didn't know how my dumb ass forgot that I had put that video on the net and she was going to damn sure see it.

"Aww, that only took a few minutes. I got hella comments on there already huh?" I replied, then smiled at her.

"Don't play with me, Marshawn." she said, while using her hands to talk, like all black women did.

"Alright, baby, I'm sorry I'm late," I apologized, then leaned across the table for a kiss. She gave me a quick peck, then started eating her salad in silence.

"Why are you not smiling? We're in the prime of our life, we are supposed to be having the time of our life," I said quoting lyrics from Kevin Gates.

"My coach wants me to move to California, so I can focus more on my game and get into some more tournaments," she spoke real low, then looked up at me with pleading eyes.

Her needing to travel all around the country all the time was the biggest issue in our relationship. It wasn't that I didn't support her career or wasn't happy for her, because I was. I knew since we were kids that this was the life she wanted for herself. I knew what I signed up for. I just hated the fact that she had to be gone a lot, sometimes a week or two at a time. Not to mention that we had a bad ass son in the picture at this point.

"I don't even know why you fixing yo' lips to tell me some shit like that. Don't no nigga determine where I lay my head, coach or not. We don't need to move nowhere, that shit sound dumb. Whenever you got a tournament down there you can just fly and come back," I told her.

Steady Mobbin'

"It's more to it than that, Marshawn. He's moving down there so he can train his son better, so he wants me to come to," she replied.

"I wouldn't give a fuck if Tiger Wood's house nigga ass wanted you to move down there, you ain't going. That shit sound dumb, move because yo' coach wants to move? Better start looking for a new coach to hire, I'll pay for it."

"Why you want to live here so bad?" she asked.

"Why do you and Spike want me to leave so bad?" I answered her with a question.

"Because we're the only ones that care about your future that's why. Portland is a trap and we need to leave before it's too late, baby," she tried to reason with me.

"Portland ain't a trap, it's home. I'm a Northeast nigga till they come and get me. When I die it's gonna be in north east, they gonna
bury me in Northeast, so goddamnit I'ma live in north east. I got the keys to the town and you want me to just pack up and leave? Leave all this money on the table? You sound dumb." I flashed on her.

"I bet I won't sound dumb when your ass is sitting in a jail cell," she shot back.

"Bosses don't go to jail," I replied arrogantly.

"Will you just think about it, for me, please? I'm ready to leave the city," she said, starting to whine now.

"Alright, queen, I'll think about it for you. You know how much I love you and can't live without you. I need you baby," I sweet talked her.

I was dead serious about loving her and her being my queen. But I was lying like a motherfucker about thinking about moving. That shit wasn't about to happen.

Midnight

It was nothing but silence and evil thoughts lurking through the air of the stolen Astro van we were in. All the guns had already been cocked back and we went over the plan a dozen

39

times. I looked over at Bobbie, he was looking out the window thinking about only God knows what. Burnside was nodding his head to a song only he could hear. When I looked behind me at Joe, he was already looking at me. He threw up G-Shine, his hood from New Jersey then started rubbing his palms together. That nigga lived for this type of shit.

Gotti was up front driving, with the AK laying on the passenger seat. Nobody ever knew what that fool was thinking.

After that video of me taking that bitch nigga shoes went viral, everybody had something to say. I mean, it was like that World War II shit, it just got social media.

Everybody was talking high power and sending death threats, the usual. A couple little Gutta Squad niggas came through the hood and shot it up. They also shot up a couple places where my lil' niggas trapped. Wasn't nothing serious though, a few legs shot on both sides. Bobbie called me and said he got the 411 on one of their main after-hours spots.

It was the perfect idea because nobody would be suspecting it. At the worst, them niggas would be expecting for us to slide through their hoods, if we even got back that night. We were coming for their pockets and we knew exactly how to do it.

"Yeah, blood, this gotta be the spot, look at all these cars parked on one block." Bobbie broke the silence.

I looked around at all the luxury cars and hooked up old schools and knew that he was right. As we drove by the house, I noticed a muscular man sitting on the porch smoking a cigarette.

"Yeah, you right, and I know the nigga on the porch too," I spoke up.

"Friend or Foe?" Burnside asked.

"Neutral, that's Z-Bo, who we went to school with."

"If he ain't friend, that means he's food. Let me get his big ass, son," Joe said.

"Gotti, bend the corner one more time and let me out right in front of this nigga. I'ma give him an ultimatum," I instructed.

Soon as we came back around the corner I jumped out with the Mossberg hanging from my shoulder. Z'Bo's eyes got wide when he saw me, then he jumped up with his hand going to his waist.

"Don't do that, Z-Bo!" I demanded, then kept walking towards him. "You see my hand ain't even on the gauge. If you make me grip it then I'ma kill you," I warned.

"Nigga, who is you?" I could tell that he was seriously debating going for it.

I walked a lil' faster closing the distance, then took my Michael Myers mask off, "It's me. O-dawg," I answered his question.

"Aww shit, just my fucking luck," he mumbled, with a look of defeat on his face.

"I just spared your life, that's if you wanna keep it. And that's only because we grew up together and you always been a standup nigga. Now, are you going to let the mob in the building or are you going to do what they pay you to do?" I asked him, while easing my hands closer to the pump.

He rubbed his head. "Man, O, you bout to go in there by yourself?"

I waved towards the van, and then Bobbie, Burnside and Jersey Joe jumped out.

"Not quite." I answered.

His eyes got back wide as he stared at the guns we were packing. They all had their mask on and exuded murderous energy. Bobbie had two .45's, Burnside had a Mac-10, and Joe was packing a Desert Eagle .50 Cal. We came to kill.

"Shid, they don't pay me enough for this shit! Y'all niggas is in the building," Z-Bo declared, almost making me laugh in his face.

"Yo', son, is we killing this nigga or what?" Joe asked.

"Naw, he was just about to hand me his 9mm and give me a layout of the place," I replied.

It took him only several minutes to tell me everything I wanted to know and hand over the piece of shit gun he had.

"Wait five minutes, then call those niggas and tell 'em we just took your pistol and ran in the spot. That way they can't trip," I instructed him, then walked through the door. We went to the left and headed down the stairs where Z-Bo claimed everybody was. I could hear all the commotion. All the talking, the dice shooting, and the glasses being slammed on the table. Take a deep breath, I know what I'm doing. I reminded myself just before we reached rock bottom.

We ran right into the so-called security guard standing to the left of the stairs, just like Z-Bo said. His eyes showed shock and surprise when he saw us.

Booyow! Booyow! Booyow!

Joe hit him close range with those 50 Cal slugs, dropping him instantly. At least his dumbass died reaching for his gun.

Blast! Blatt! Boom! Boom! Boom! Blaat!

Burnside and Bobbie filled the other guard up with holes, just as he was getting ready to start busting.

Boc! Boc!

At least he got to go out shooting. That was two crash dummies down and one more to go.

I looked around for the third guard, but he wasn't at his post. It seemed like time had frozen at that moment. Everybody was stuck staring at me while I was scanning the room. They all had the look of fear written on their faces. I believe they were all hoping that they weren't the next victim of my hit squad.

Kaboom!

I put one in the air to snap them out of there daze and let them hear the sound of death that the Mossberg makes. They all screamed and put their hands over their heads to the block any pellets from raining on them.

"The next one move, knock the soul out of somebody, nigga or bitch. I want two things and I want both of them in the next five seconds or everybody dyin'. I want everybody to lay flat on their stomach with ya arms spread, and I want to know who's the third security guard," I stated very calmly, but with venom in my voice.

Steady Mobbin'

Everybody immediately hit the floor and looked in the direction of a guy laying down by the bar. They didn't want to point him out, but they damn sure gave him up. When he seen that everybody was looking at him that's when he decided to stand up. I could see the bulge under his shirt, but I wasn't worried about that, he knew that was kamikaze.

I made my way over to him slowly, enjoying the buildup, knowing everybody was watching me. I stood face to face with him for a few seconds before saying, "You from Gutta Squad?" I asked

"Naw, I just work for Butta, I don't bang," he said.

I stared through his eyes trying to get a read on him. A nigga will lie to his own his mama when staring death in the eyes. After deciding that I believed him, I took his gun from him, and then I turned around to face the crowd.

"Listen up, because I'm only going to say this one time and one time only. From now on, anybody caught gambling or hanging out at any of the Gutta Squad spots will be killed on site. Tonight, though, everybody's going home and we ain't gon rob y'all. Now, is there anybody from Gutta Squad in here?" When nobody answered, I turned back to the so-called guard and pulled my mask up.

"Do y'all know who I am?" I asked in a tone above a whisper. He nodded his head like I knew he would. "You're going to take my man upstairs to that safe and hand that money over. If you play dumb or act like you don't know the combination then I'ma kill you and everybody in this room, you understand?" He nodded again, "Now give me your gun and get back here in forty-five seconds," I demanded.

He gave me a 9 mm then lead Bobbie upstairs to the money. I analyzed the piece of shit gun, popped the clip out, then tossed it across the room. I ain't gone lie, I did all the shit for dramatics, I loved an audience.

"Now the rest of you, I'm leaving all y'all with ya money and jewels. Whatever money you got on the table or floor or whatever, y'all can sort that out when I leave. I'm doing this in good faith to show that the mob don't got no issues with y'all. But if you're trippin', then come holla at the mob life because we bout that life," I said, then looked over at the two dead niggas.

Bobbie came back holding a large duffel bag, so I felt it was time to blow that joint.

"We Gucci?" I asked.

"We good," he replied.

I yanked out the banger I took from Z-Bo and aimed it right at the bitch ass guard's face. "You ready to die?" I asked.

"Don't kill me, man," he said, while raising his hands in the air.

Boc! Boc!

Face shot and a chest shot, then he crumbled to the floor. I stood over him to make sure he was no longer. Yeah, he was dead. I remember staring into his lifeless eyes, then the saying popped into my head 'if you die with them open that mean you deserved it.'

Boc! Boc! Boc!

I gave him those extra ones in the chest because clearly, he deserved it. I wonder will I die with my eyes open?

"Y'all wait five minutes then do whatever y'all want," I said as we made our exit.

I looked to the left and saw our van parked by the corner, but something told me to look right. I saw three niggas rushing down the street, headed straight to us. We were frozen for a split second and in that second, I recognized just the niggas I wanted to see. Gucci Ty always stood out with those two long signature braids that he always rocked. I found out later that the other two niggas were Pull-Out and Ron, the pussies who ran in the spot on me.

Boc! Boc! Boc! Boc! Boc! Click, click!

I set it off, but then the nine was empty and it was on.

Boom! Boom! Boom! Boca! Boca! Blaatt! Blaat! Blaat! Boc! Boc! Boc! Boc!

44

Steady Mobbin'

Everybody started shooting at one time and spreading out in the street. I threw that wack ass 9mm on the ground and went to work with the pump.

Kaboom! Kaboom!

I ran for cover behind a car. I wasn't with that standing in the open shit.

Boom! Boom! Boca! Bloca! Blocka!

"What's happenin', cuz?" one of those niggas said, while hitting the car I was hiding behind.

I jumped up but couldn't focus on nobody because it was too dark and all I saw was flame. Kaboom! I let one off just for the fuck of it.

Boc! Boc! Blaat! Blaat!

"Y'all get out the way!" somebody screamed out.

I was about to look, then it hit me whose voice that was, so I got lower cause I knew what was coming.

Bloocca! Bloocca! Bloocca! Bloocca! Bloocca! Bloocca! Bloocca! Bloocca!

Once Gotti start letting that AK go off it was a wrap. That bitch owned the night, I couldn't hear nothing else. It felt like he was shooting for an hour when it was actually less than ten seconds. I broke to the van while those bitch niggas ran the other way. Yeah, that was a good day and night, I'll never forget that shit.

Marcellus Allen

Chapter 4
May 4th

I see dead bodies every time I close my eyes/getting' money, known to whip ten pies at a time/so muthafuck the law, I'ma get this paper/and hold court in the streets like I'm Larry Davis! /I think I'm Larry Davis! I feel like Larry Davis! /money in the 'frigerator, now they know we gettin' paper! /Larry Davis!

I had to pause from working on my song after my son jumped off the couch yelling Larry Davis! To this day, that's one of my best memories. I smile every time I think about it.

I was posted up in my home studio working on a song called 'Larry Davis' that I was planning on making my next street anthem. My bad ass son had snuck his way into the room like he always did whenever he heard me recording. He always did the same special opp's move when he came in too. Shit was pure comedy. He would come in walking real slow towards the couch like I couldn't see him, with a smile on his face. Then once he got on the couch, I'd look at him and he'd hide his face. He does it every time.

"You like that, Mar-Mar?" I asked him while laughing. The lil' nigga wasn't wearing no clothes. Just a diaper and my Cincinnati Red's hat that he stole off the couch.

"Larry Davis! Daddy!" he shouted, then started trying to dance and fell down.

"Come here, lil' nigga," I said while picking him up. "You gone be the realist nigga to ever walk this earth, you hear me?" I told him, while looking him deep in the eyes.

"I wanna see," he replied, while trying to take my chains off my neck.

"Hold on, nigga," I said then put him back down. "Here you go." I put my two Jesus pieces around his neck.

"Larry Davis, Daddy!" he shouted while jumping up and down gripping my pieces.

"Aight, I got you," I responded, then hit play turning back on the hook.

Me and my lil' man was rocking out to the song for another five minutes before Olay came in hatin' like always. She stood there for a few seconds watching our son and trying not to laugh. Mar-Mar jumped up and down rapping with my chains on was a sight to see. He must have felt her presence or seen me looking at her, because he turned around real slow like he was expecting to see her.

"Help me, Daddy!" he shouted, then ran to me with his arms out.

I picked my lil' nigga up then stopped the music. "Why you killin' the vibe?" I asked her.

"No, why do you have him in here listening to all this cussing and talking about he Larry Davis?" she turned it around on me.

"First off, it's just my hook on repeat and it's only one cuss word, and he don't know who the hell Larry Davis is," I responded.

"Good, and I wanna keep it that way, Marshawn. Get over here, Mar-Mar," she said.

He buried his face in my chest. "Man, leave my son alone. We in here chillin'. You just jealous. Today is about to be father/son day, so fall back," I told her.

"You said you were taking me somewhere today. What happened to that?" she asked with an attitude.

"Mar-Mar, go find some clothes that you want ya mama to dress you in," I told my son, then put him down.

He tried to run past Olay, but she snatched my hat off his head before he could make it out. When he was safe in the hall, he turned around and stuck his tongue out while lifting my chains up. That lil nigga is hilarious, real talk. Olay acted like she was about to chase him and that nigga was gone.

She put her hand on her hip and twisted her neck, then said, "So, you just gone get me all excited for no reason?"

"Don't I always come through for you, baby?"

"I don't know, you tell me!" she shot back.

"I'd rather show you than tell you," I told her and then took her hands.

I walked her to our full-length mirror in our bedroom then wrapped my arms around her. "You look so beautiful."

"Thank you," she responded.

"Aight, you know how they do it in the movies and shit. Who am I to mess tradition up? Cover your eyes with your hands." I lifted her hands up.

I went to the closet and grabbed my Gucci bag then dropped it at her feet. "Don't look yet," I said after I caught her trying to peek. I grabbed a Tiffany box out the bag then took the necklace out. Soon as the ice touched her skin, she took a deep breath in. "It's cold huh? Yeah, that's that real ice."

After I was done dripping her neck, I grabbed the other blue box out the bag and pulled out the bracelet.

"Give me your arm," I said then took her arm and put the ice on her wrist.

She opened her eyes before I told her to and her eyes got wide as she stared at the butterfly necklace I bought her. "Oh my God," she yelled, then covered her mouth with her right hand and that's when she seen the bracelet.

"They're so beautiful! Thank you, baby!" she yelled again, then jumped on me.

"Oh, now I'm the man, huh?" I teased her.

"You're always the man, daddy," she answered, then started sticking her tongue down my throat.

I palmed her ass and she got to grinding on me getting my dick hard as a missile. "I got somethin' else for you, baby." I tried to put her down, but she wasn't having it.

"Give it to me later. Right now, I want some dick." She gripped my meat.

"I got you tonight, baby, I promise," I said, then finally managed to peel her off me.

"It's been a week, Marshawn!" she pouted and crossed her arms like a baby.

Instead of responding to her, I reached back into the bag and got to pulling out knots of money. "Here." I handed the money to her.

"What's this for? You want me to count it and put it up for you?"

I laughed. "Naw, that's for you to go shoppin' with today. That's thirteen bands. Get a full body massage, hair and nails did, then go get some clothes and bags. Oh, make sure you go grab some outfits from Victoria's Secret too."

"Okay, thank you, daddy," she said with the brightest smile on her face.

"You deserve it, Queen. Now can you go get my son dressed so I can blow this joint?"

"Okay." She left the room still smiling, but not before I tapped her on the ass.

I loved seeing my baby happy and it was even better when I was the one making her smile. Real shit, I never deserved Olay, she was too pure and too innocent. The only reason she ended up with a real street nigga was because we grew up in church together. That was a good moment though, a real bright spot in my life. That's a period I wish I could have held on to cause the darker days were coming.

Hours later

I got to the studio and wasn't nobody there but Rugar, which was normal cause he practically lived there.

"Mobbin', nigga!" I greeted him.

"Shit, just workin' on some new beats. I see you brought lil O-Dawg with you," he replied, while shaking me up.

"Yeah, I gave wifey the day off."

"What's up, lil' bad nigga?" he greeted my son, giving him dap.

"Sup, nigga?" my son said back to him, taking his sucker out of his mouth.

Steady Mobbin'

"Go find somethin' to do, lil boy," I said, then walked over to the computers to check out what Rugar had going on.

He had a pretty dope beat playing, but it was a little too fast for my flow. I had that slow Pusha T type of flow. I saw he had a double cup of that lean just sitting there, so I snatched it up and got my sip on. I was never big on the drugs or drank, but every now and then I'd get faded. I liked lean, though. I loved being on that turtle time. I barely did it though, cause it was real where I was at, shootings every day. I couldn't afford to be moving slow.

"You fuckin' with this one?" he asked me.

"Naw, I need somethin' a lil bit slower with more base in it. You know I be tryna' bring them bars out," I answered, then took another sip.

"You want somethin' for that Larry Davis hook you sent me or you wanna keep that Ross beat?"

"Make somethin' for me, but I wanna hear somethin' soulful right now."

"I got one just for you," he said, then got to searching through his files.

I took another sip, then walked over to my son. He wasn't worried about nothing we had going on. His focus was on some video game, I'm sure I bought him.

"You good, Mar-Mar?" I asked.

"Yup!" he answered, without taking his eyes off that game.

"Can I have my chains back now?"

"Nooo!" he whined, then grabbed the chains and held them against his chest trying to protect them.

"Yo', tell me what you think about this one," Rugar called over to me.

Soon as the beat dropped, I knew it was the one. It started off with an old school sample, some lady singing the hook. Then that 808 kicked in and it was a wrap. The beat had a real depressing dark side to it, the type that I loved. I stood there nodding my head for minutes, just feeling it. I had Rugar play the beat back three different times before I had my first couple of bars.

"Forgive me Lord, that Blood Money I couldn't ignore/Black Panther deep in my heart, I'd rather be Mutulu Shakur/Extension on the A-K it's long as a cord/Mind frame of a millionaire, so every thought is a porch/of course, I'm from the North-East side where it's die or kill/I grew up sellin' pillz on the same corner where Turk got killed."

I spit that to Rugar, then tried to get back in my zone, so I could finish the verse, but he wasn't going for it.

"Aye, go record that real quick, so we don't lose it. That shit was hot, nigga."

"I'm not about to forget it, blood. I wrote it in my head," I responded.

"Just record it real quick and we'll loop it and let it play while we work on the rest," he insisted.

I ended up giving in and recording the bars that I had, then we sat around freestyling for an hour trying to get three solid verses.

"You know what songs you performing tomorrow night?" he asked, breaking me out of my zone.

I was scheduled to perform at the Roseland for the Cinco De Mayo festival that next night. Every year that was the most poppin' night of the year. Downtown was packed to capacity all night. There was bitches everywhere, which meant all the niggas were going to be there, which meant it was triv every year.

"Well you already know I gotta do 'Money Must be the Reason,' even though I'm tired of that song," I said.

"Of course," he responded.

"I think I'ma do that 'Bullets with Ya Name' and I'll do that 'You're the Only one,' for the bitches."

"That sounds like a go," he agreed.

I looked over at my son, who was staring dead at us, being nosey. His lil bad ass nodded at us, then picked back up his game. Me and Rugar looked at each other and started dying. My lil man was something else. About twenty minutes later, Bobbie walked in with a brown paper bag and tossed it to my son.

"That's blood money, lil nigga," he said as if my son knew what he meant.

"How much?" I asked, as we shook each other up.

"Twenty-two from last night," he answered non chalantly.

I nodded then tried to get back in my zone. I watched my son dump all that money in his lap and start playing with it. My mind flashed back to that night before, me standing over that nigga shooting him those extra times.

'Blood money in my son's hands from his father's sins/I'm just hoping he don't end up like his father and friends/'nuff money in his trust fund to buy his father a Benz/sold my soul to the devil just to buy some rims/My mama ask how I sleep with these murders on my conscience/I told her like a baby, and does that make me a monster?/

I spit that off the dome and got to thinking how true that shit was. I remember the looks on those niggas faces, that shit hit them niggas deep. I already knew Rugar would beg me to record it, so I just walked in the booth and got it out the way. When I came out, Bobbie was staring at me and rubbing his chin.

"What's on yo mind, nigga?" I asked.

"Blood, you should just slide to Atlanta and get it poppin' with this music shit. You can really take it there."

"You too, huh? Don't trip, I'ma take it there from right here in North-East," I shot back.

"This street shit gone be the death of us," he predicted.

The way he said it gave me goose bumps for some reason. It wasn't a question or theory, it was a prophecy. The shit came natural to us, like night and day.

"I don't plan on dying soon, nigga, just know that. I love the streets, I'ma gangsta, this all I know. Get money, fuck bitches and pop crabs. What else is there to do? Man, we got too much money to get killed by these broke ass Portland niggas. They're just mere mortals, remember that," I said in the most arrogant way possible.

Marcellus Allen

He looked at me with excitement in his eyes. I put that battery in his back. I know he was feeling me.

Hours Later

I opened my front door a lil after midnight and was surprised when I didn't see Olay sitting on the couch. She called me a couple times, hours ago, telling me to get Mar-Mar home. So, I already knew she was gone be hot at me. I looked at my lil nigga as I made my way to his room. I could never get over how much he looked like me. That lil boy looked like we were twins.

I laid him in his crib then took my chains off his ass. He fell in love with them that day, so I told myself I had to buy him his own ASAP 'cause he wasn't about to be robbing me. When I turned around, Olay was standing by the door, butt ass naked. I looked her up and down and noticed she had got her nails and feet done. I was expecting her to be looking mad, but instead, she had a look of seduction on her face. She motioned for me to follow her with her finger then walked out of the room.

My dick got hard as a muthafucka as I followed behind her, watching her switch down the hall. When I got inside the bedroom, she was standing by the bed with one leg cocked up on it rubbing her clit.

"So, I guess you're not mad at me?" I said, while taking my clothes off.

"Tomorrow, I'ma cuss you out for keeping my son out all night. Tonight, you bout to eat my pussy and fuck me," she answered. She sped the pace up on her clit while keeping eye contact.

"Taste *my* pussy," I told her as I stood face to face with her.

She stuck her fingers in her mouth and started sucking on them, making it slurp. After that, I dropped on my knees and got to going to work with my tongue. I opened them pretty lips up and licked   laps all around them walls. She was moaning out some shit I couldn't understand and grinding her hips. After a few moments of that, I decided it was time to take her there. I

54

locked on to that clit and got to suckin' on it like my life depended on it.

"Oh! Oh! Daddy!" she moaned out then gripped the back of my head. The more pressure I applied, the more she grinded and moaned out. "I'm bout to cum, daddy!" she screamed, then tried to mush my face inside her pussy.

I kept sucking on that magic button until she got to shaking and cumming all in my mouth. When she released my head, that's when I knew she was done. I licked up all her juices from around that pussy and even the streaks down her legs. When I was done feasting, I stood up eye to eye with her, dick poking her in the stomach.

"So, you wanna get fucked right?"

"I want you to beat it up."

I lifted her in the air by the ass. She wrapped her legs and arms around me tight. She knew what time it was. I slid in her real slow making her gasp and bury her face in my neck while she tried to muffle her moans.

"What you hiding for? You wanna get pounded out right?" I taunted her.

She bit my neck then I really went to work on her. I fucked her in every position that night, that I knew of, making her cum multiple times. For some weird reason as I laid in the bed that night, I kept thinking about my lyrics from earlier that day.

I kept picturing my son playing with the money that I killed a nigga for. I wondered to myself was I cursing my son by doing that shit. I had said in that song that I sold my soul to the devil, did I really? I flashed back to me shooting that nigga those extra times cause his eyes were open. I went to sleep that night wondering would I die with my eyes open! Did I deserve that?

Marcellus Allen

Steady Mobbin'

Chapter 5
May 5th (Cinco De Mayo)

"Yeah, this is Big O-Dawg from the Mob, just in case y'all bitch ass niggas act like ya don't recognize a supreme being! We live from the Lloyd Center, about fifteen deep, ya know, buying what the fuck we want while y'all hiding in ya houses," I spoke into the camera on my lil' niggas I-Phone.

It was Cinco de Mayo, the day of my performance at the Roseland and we were turnt up! At that moment we were tearing the mall up, buying everything, being loud and getting at every bitch we saw. In the midst of all that, the lil homie, Tre, pulled out his phone and started recording us. Anytime a camera was on me, I showed the fuck out!

"And when the Reaper catch you niggas, I'ma send you to where the rest of ya bitch ass dead homies are at! Word is bond, Slime!" Jersey Joe jumped in front of the camera.

We all took turns talking our shit and throwing up gang signs and yelling free our homies, until we made it to Foot Locker. It seemed as if we were all of one mind as soon as we saw the sign, to rush the store.   The few white people that were in there made their way to the exit, fast. As I think back on it, we were a sight to see. A bunch of young wild niggas with jewels on, yelling and shit. Joe walked right up to the two women behind the cash registers. One was Black and the other was White.

"Yo, ma, how you doing? You know who we are or what?" The nigga let that be the first words out his mouth.

"Uhhh, I don't think so," the Black one answered, sounding unsure.

"I feel disrespected. How you not gone recognize the richest niggas in the city? I should buy this whole store. Shut y'all down a few weeks." Burnside jumped in, leaning on the counter.

I shook my head at these burnt out niggas and   looked for some Jordan's to add to my collection. I was already fly as a muthafucka, but I can't ever have too much gear. Shit, I had on so much designer gear, I probably looked out of place. I was rockin' some Balmain jeans, red Gucci hoody with shite Gucci logo and some red and white hi-top Gucci shoes. I think it goes without saying that I had the Gucci belt on display.

I found the Jordan Retro eights and the Olympic Sevens I was looking for and told the worker dude that I needed them in size eleven. I looked around and saw everybody grabbing shoes and still talkin' shit on camera. We had it looking like a swap meet in there! Bobbie was posted by the door watching everything move outside the store. Lil short ass nigga was always mean muggin' with his fist balled up.

"Yo, Bobbie, ain't nobody in here, nigga," I called out to him.

"Blood, you never know when you gotta kill somebody," he said then turned back around.

I looked at Gotti who was looking at me with the same facial expression.

"What's wrong with ya mans'?" I playfully asked.

"Pshh, that's yo best friend, nigga," he shot back.

I made my way to the counter, so I could cop my kicks and blow that joint. Those two fools were still at the counter trying to spit game. I bumped those niggas out the way and pulled out way more money than necessary.

"Excuse me, ladies. I just wanna buy these shoes and then I'll be out y'all's way!" I said, while giving them all twenty-six teeth.

"Umm, aren't you a rapper?" the Black one asked, then looked at her friend for confirmation.

I smiled again. "Yeah, I rap. My name is O-Dawg," I answered all cocky-like. They knew who I was when I stepped in that bitch.

"Aww, nigga, they only knew who you was cause you always on Instagram with ya shirt off and shit! They know who the real muscle is," Burnside said trying to be funny.

"You know what, son? I'm buying the whole top rack now, word to mutha!" Joe jumped in sounding sarcastic but was dead serious. "A yo, my man's! I want that whole top row right there!" he told the worker who had brought my shoes out for me.

I burst out laughing at the man's facial expression at Joe's request. We were definitely giving them a show. I read the two women's name tags, Joy and Sarah.

"Joy, make sure you give this crazy East Coast nigga yo' number. He went hard for it. We got a show tonight at the Roseland. Maybe he'll bring you to the V.I.P.," I said, then got my shoes and blew that joint.

We roamed the mall for some women for another ten minutes, minus Burnside and Joe 'cause they were loading up their cars with shoes due to their high sighting. That's when we spotted some bitch crabs at the food court.

"I know that's not them niggas, blood," Gotti broke the silence.

"Hold up, don't nobody do nothin'," I said, then pulled my phone out calling Burnside. "Blood, we caught these crabs up here at the food court right now! Where y'all at? Aight, come from the McDonalds side," I said, then hung up and faced my goons. "It might be more of those niggas on that side over there. They bout to check it out," I told them.

We stood there for a few minutes trying to blend in and watching these niggas. It was Dirty Dan, Half-Dead and his baby mama, Felicia, the one Burnside was fuckin'. They were sitting there eating McDonalds and shit like they didn't have a care in the world. It seemed weird that it was only two of those niggas in there. I thought they had more niggas with them somewhere. Either that, or they both had two guns on 'em.

They must have sensed the presence of danger 'cause they eventually looked our way, both of them at the same time. I know their hearts dropped. They hurried up and looked away with hopes that we wouldn't notice them, but no dice! I watched Half-Dead steal a few glances our way while he made some calls on his phone. At that moment, I knew they were by themselves and most likely left their guns in the car. Everybody always left their burners in the car when coming to that hot ass mall. Niggas stayed catching cases in there. Either mall security was jamming people up or their P O was in there trippin'.

We left our guns in the cars too, that's why we were Mobbin' deep, though. Soon as we headed in their direction, they got up and tried to make their exit.

"Aye, Half-Dead, you a bitch nigga!" I yelled at him.

"Come catch the fade outside then, nigga. It's whatever!" he yelled back, while walking backwards.

I don't know who that crab thought he was fooling with that shit, but that was the oldest move in the book. It was actually quite entertaining, but the funniest part was when he was walking backwards with his arms in the air. Dirty Dan got rocked off on by Joe!

Dirty Dan hit the ground from the first punch and Half-Dead turned around right in time to take one to the jaw. He stayed on his feet though, and got to throwin' those thangs with my nigga, to his credit.

We all sprinted over there fast as we could to get our licks in. Half-Dead's baby mama, Felicia, was just standing there watching those niggas go at it, When Joe snuffed her off her feet. She was snoring before she even hit the ground. That shit was funny!

Bobbie, Gotti, and like four more of my niggas rushed Half-Dead and got him on the ground. The rest of the Mob started stomping Dirty Dan out!

"Bitch ass nigga! Talk that shit now!" I growled, as I joined the party stomping Half-Dead out.

I was hitting his bitch ass with the bags in my hand and was kicking the shit out of him! When the lil nigga started recording it, that's when we really turned it up! We pounded on those pussies until mall security came rushing over, then we ran out.

When we tried to back out of the parking spot, it was three of those rent-a-cops blocking our path. At that point they had taken shit too far. Who the fuck did they really believe they were? Like we were just gone sit there until the real police showed up!

Steady Mobbin'

I jumped out with the .40 cal in my hand and the look of murder on my face. "Y'all bitch ass niggas better get out the way before I yank y'all. We ran from y'all in there cause we know y'all only doing your jobs, but now y'all making it personal," I told them, then started walking up on them. They moved out the way, so I jumped back in and mashed out.

Later that night

We were posted up in the parking lot of the Roseland theater, smoking, drinking and putting on a show until it was time to do my show. It was packed outside so we were in full fledge stunt mode. We had those European whips right on display, doors open with the stereos on the max. Everybody was leanin' on their shit, calling over women from out the line, parking lot pimpin'.

I was sitting on the hood of my car with Tamia standing in between my legs, so I couldn't get at none of the broads out there. I wasn't trippin' off that anyways. I had money on the way and a show to do. I ain't gone lie, I had it on thick! I was just sitting there with my Michael Myers mask on, nodding my head to the music. Couldn't nobody see my face but they all knew who the white on white 750 I was sitting on belonged to; they knew it belonged to me.

"Ain't that him right there, daddy?" Tamia asked me, nodding in the direction of the nigga that was walking towards us.

"Yeah! Grab that bag," I told her.

She went and popped the trunk and grabbed the bag as Premo made his way over. They exchanged bags real quick, her throwing the new one in the trunk, and then she came back between my legs.

"Damn, nigga, you just out here with the mask on though?" Premo started laughing.

"You just gone be out here with a whole brick on you? It's a lot of wolves out here," I replied, then swept my arms at the packed parking lot.

"The only wolves out here is yo' niggas. The rest of these clowns are just here for the show. Plus, I'm willing to die about it." He touched his hip, showing me that he was strapped.

"Say that then," I said, unimpressed. Everybody always claimed they were ready to die, until they were staring in that barrel. If niggas wanted that dope off him, then he was gone give it up, but he was in the presence of a killer and a bad bitch. So, he had no choice but to show his nuts.

"Let me get up outta here though cause this shit is hot and the boys might pull up any second from now."

We dapped each other up. "Hit me when it's heavy," I told him as he walked away.

He turned around. "Oh, I saw that shit on the gram from the mall earlier. Y'all niggas be safe," he warned.

I just nodded my head, wasn't nothing to discuss. My heart and chest were full of arrogance and pride, so I wasn't worried about nothing. That's the thing with power, it made me feel untouchable.

"His gun probably ain't even cocked back talkin' bout he ready to die," Tamia said, out of nowhere.

"The nigga will shoot, I'll give 'em that, but he ain't bout to die over no dope."

"Would you? If you had your gun?" she asked.

"If I can go for my gun in any situation, then I'm reaching, but if they got the drop, then they got that. Niggas better leave all that dyin' for my chain shit to those fake ass rappers. I can guarantee ain't no niggas in Portland just gone try and rob me," I responded.

"Why you say that?"

I took my mask off, "Cause they know they're better off killing me than robbing me and letting me live. Niggas know if they want these jewels, they come with a funeral. Mines or theirs," I told her, while staring her in the eyes.

Steady Mobbin'

I always kept it real with my bitches. They knew what type of nigga I was. I kept it a hunnid, and they loved it. I palmed her ass, pulling her closer to me, then stuck my tongue in her mouth.

We stood there kissing and touching for a few moments until she squeezed my dick saying, "You should give me some dick in the car real quick."

The way she purred in my ear and was massaging my meat, had me strongly debating it. "We ain't got time. Plus, them niggas on the way over here."

"Well, you need to make some time for me real soon."

"If you want, you can go home and make sure it's twenty-eight bands in that bag and I'll be there when I'm done," I offered.

"Nigga, please, I wish I would. Ain't no bitch getting no action at you tonight but me, don't try me," she shut that down really quick, like I knew she would.

Gotti and Bobbie walked up after talking to security, so I knew it was that time. It seemed like they were over there negotiating for over ten minutes, I stood there waiting for the bill.

"Yo, O, they trippin' like a muthafucka over there. You know niggas don't never got no heats up in here so they really on their bully right now," Gotti said.

"So, what they talkin'?" I was getting irritated already.

"They said only one gun and it's gone cost a rack," he told me.

"Blood, we should just push the line on their bitch asses. Just walk past 'em with the smacks. What the fuck they gone do?" Bobbie jumped in.

I thought about it for a second weighing the options, then decided to go along. It wasn't like security was lying, nobody ever got in with bangers. The Roseland was a death trap though. If somebody played their cards right, it was the only way in and one way out, through the same doors. The only exception was, if you were performing, you got to use the back door.

"Naw, it's gucci. I'll pay it. It ain't like we gone have some enemies in here and if we did, they damn sho' ain't have no smacks. Let's get this money, grab some bitches and blow this joint." I made the decision.

By the time I finished my sentence, the rest of the crew had walked up and caught the end of it. We were deep as shit, plus I was gone be the one with the banger, so I wasn't trippin'.

"Hold on, son, so we all leaving our guns in the car?" Jersey Joe needed clarification.

"I know you ain't scared, nigga!" Burnside taunted.

"Yo, word is bond. I done took souls with my bare hands, son. They don't call me the East Coast Grim Reaper for no reason."

"I've never heard nobody else but yourself call you that dumb shit. Stop showing off for your new date before I slap you," Burnside got on him.

That's when I looked at the girl hugged up on him more closely. It was Joy. She didn't even look twenty-one, but she was looking sexy. She had that look of infatuation in her eyes and I knew what that meant. She had never been around real niggas like us. She was a square. Hindsight is 20/20, but I should have killed her then.

We got right, then headed to the back entrance, the V.I.P. door. Soon as we got to the door, one of the fake ass guards put his hand on my chest. I looked at it like it was covered in shit, then up to his eyes.

"If you don't take yo' dirty ass hand off this thousand-dollar hoody, I'ma put you on tonight's news." He removed it immediately. "Now, you know exactly who the fuck I am and what the deal is," I pulled the band out my pocket and watched his partner nod at him before he took it.

We made it to the V.I.P. room without any other incidents and it was poppin' in there. Everybody had a blunt in their mouth and a bitch in their face. All eyes were sizing us up and we were doing the same thing. It wasn't no threats in there though, just a bunch of rap niggas covered in tattoos.

Steady Mobbin'

My nigga, T-Soprano, spotted me and made his way over with some of his lil niggas. Soprano wasn't no rap nigga, he was a real nigga that knew how to rap like me.

"What's good with my Mob nigga, though?" T-Soprano greeted me with his signature line for me.

"Shit, what's mobbin' with my Twelfth Avenue nigga, though?" I responded with my signature line, then gave my nigga a G hug.

"Gettin' ready to go hit this stage then head to the after party. Y'all slidin' through?"

"These niggas all from yo hood?" I asked.

"Yeah, they with the Ave.," he said, then introduced all his goons to us. We all shook up and broke the lil tension.

"We probably gone slide through. I'll get the info before we leave," I told him, then made my way to the couch.

Tamia sat right on my lap, but I wasn't trippin', that was expected. "Put this in yo' purse," I told her, then handed her my .45 with the thirty clips. The nigga sitting on the couch across from us seen it and started looking all nervous and shit. Like I had said, rap niggas with tattoos.

"Aye, fam, you tryna' hit the weed?" he extended the blunt to me.

I looked from him to his bitch, then back to him. "Good looking, blood." I took it then passed it to Bobbie. "Y'all can kill it, that's on the house," I told him.

He started smirking, then hit the blunt a few times. When he was done coughing, he said, "This some fire. I'm bout to see if Gotti wanna hit it." Then he got up.

I watched the guy on the couch bitch look at him with contempt, then back to me. "So, what's up, blood? What hood you from?" I asked him.

"Oh, I don't bang, bro. I just get money," he gave the typical bitch nigga answer.

I looked him up and down and at all the costume jewelry he was wearing.

"I can tell," I said, being sarcastic.

"I'll be right back, baby," he told his girl. Then looked at me. "Excuse me, fam." Then he made his exit.

She was looking at him funny the whole time like the lame that he was. I would have been highly surprised if the nigga came back. I figured he was gone text her or something' after about ten minutes or so.

"Daddy, why you messing with him like that?" Tamia asked after kissing me.

"Cause the nigga was sitting here portraying to be a real nigga and shit. I hate when rap niggas be making money off of shit we really out here doing. I really got homies laying in the dirt behind this shit. He lucky I ain't take his fake ass jewelry and if you weren't here, I'd take his bitch," I was being cocky as usual, but truthful.

She punched me in the chest. "I'd kill yo ass, nigga, don't try me," she said.

I noticed how baby girl was all in my mouth, but I kept looking away every time I made eye contact with her. I thought about getting at her on the low but then a better idea came to mind.

"Yo, sweetheart, what's your name?" I asked, and soon as I did Tamia turned around on my lap, so she could face her. I felt her tense up like she was just waiting to jump.

"Uhh, Chaniece," she answered sounding all shy and shit.

"A woman is a reflection of her nigga, but something tells me that you're nothing like him. You do know he's a sucka and he ain't coming back, right?"

She looked around for him to no avail.

"He said he was," she weakly responded.

"Listen, you're a beautiful chocolate sister, don't waste your youth on a bitch nigga. It's bad for your skin. I can see that you like light skinned niggas covered in tatt's. I got you, don't trip," I told her.

I looked around the room until I found my lil nigga, Trell. He was the perfect match for her.

"Yo, Trell, come here, blood!" I yelled to him.

Steady Mobbin'

"What's good, big bro?" he asked, then came over and looked at us.

"Chaniece's man felt intimidated by us and left her all alone. I figured you would wanna get to know her since she likes light, bright niggas with tatts." I told him, trying not to laugh.

He looked her up and down a few times with a look of satisfaction, then sat down right next to her.

"Don't worry about that lame nigga no more. You about to fuck with a real nigga," he told her, then got closer in her face. Really getting on her.

Tamia turned back to me. "Ugh, why y'all Mob Life niggas so cocky? It's irritating," she rolled her eyes at me.

"Cause, we them niggas, that's why. You know what's up. I stay gettin' yo panties wet, so don't start frontin' now."

"Pshh, whatever, nigga." She sucked her teeth then looked back at them talking. My lil nigga had her all smiles and shit already. They would make a lil cute couple though.

"Yeah, that's my good deed for the year. So, don't ask me for shit. Real niggas are hard to find out here," I joked with her.

A couple security guards came over to tell me it was show time in five minutes. So, I got up to gather the troops. By the time I found everybody, they were already calling me to the stage. When I got to the curtains, I moved 'em to the side a lil to see how packed it was out there. It was packed! A jolt of nervousness shot through my body. Take a deep breath, I know what I'm doing, I reminded myself.

"Let's go, nigga!" Burnside said, then pushed me forward.

Somebody passed me a mic and it was on. The nervousness was replaced with arrogance as I gripped the mic even tighter. I ran on stage with my niggas following right behind me. The crowd started roaring as soon as we stepped foot on stage. That was the feeling that drove me the most, the energy that I thrived off. As I looked into the crowd, it seemed like every single set of eyes were on me. I loved it.

"When I say Mob, y'all say Life!" I screamed, ready to get this shit live.

"Mob!" I yelled.

"Life!" they chanted back.

"Mob!" I yelled again.

"Life!"

"That's what the fuck I'm talkin' about! Show a real nigga some love! Yo, DJ, you know what the people want! Drop that *Money Must Be the Reason*," I commanded.

The crowd got even louder when they heard that beat drop. The whole town loved that song. *'Money must be the reason must be the reason/why the cars are European and all the diamonds freezing/why they committing treason and snitchin' every season/they hate it that I'm breathin', but I'ma die squeezin'/so money must be the reason ... know it's the reason!*

The whole crowd was singing the hook with me and Bobbie, word for word, that shit was crazy. The hook was real melodic, so it was easy for everybody to just vibe to it. Once we got to the verses it was all the way turnt up and we were all running across the stage just feeling ourselves. Before I started the third verse, I seen a crowd of niggas bullying their way to the front.

I had a gut feeling who they were before I could even see them clearly, but when they made it to the front, my hand automatically went to my waist out of habit, but of course, it was no gun there. I kept on rapping while looking those bitch niggas in the eyes, one by one. It looked like the whole Gutta Squad was in that building. It had to be thirty of those niggas, real shit. Butta's fat ass was just standing there with his arms folded like he was some type of Teflon don or something. I wanted to kill that nigga right then on the spot!

Him, Gucci Ty, Dirty Dan, Half-Dead, Pressha, Pull-Out and Ron were all standing in front just daring us to try something. I looked at Bobbie who was throwing the hood up on them niggas, while the rest of the goons were flashing gun signs and gang signs.

After the song was done, that's when I decided to join the bullshit.

"When I say Mob, y'all say Life! Mob!" I yelled.

68

Steady Mobbin'

"Life!" the crowd screamed back.

"Mob!" I yelled again.

"LIFE!" They yelled back even louder.

"That's what the fuck I'm talkin' about! The Mob in the building like always. It's a couple bitch ass niggas right here I see! I wanna let y'all know summin' right now. Whoever bring me one of those fake ass Gutta Squad chains, I'ma pay 'em ten bands on the spot! When y'all see one of the pussies, just take they chain and call me ASAP!" I declared.

The crowd got hella hyped at my declaration. It got so loud I had to stop talking for a minute.

Those ho ass niggas were grabbing their chains and lifting them in the air so the crowd could see them. They definitely were putting on a show. I 'll give them that.

"You come take it, bitch ass nigga!" Pull-Out yelled, when the crowd got silent.

Instead of responding, I walked up to the DJ and told him what song to play then went back center stage. When it dropped, the crowd went ham soon as they heard the beat. It was on.

"Location!? ... Roseland Theater, those chumps right there in the front, they know not to come up here fuckin' wit' no real niggas!" I yelled soon as War Pain dropped.

Those niggas' faces went from having fun, to dead ass serious in a heartbeat. I walked closer to Half-Dead, then started to back up.

"Mood? My nigga, Burnside, dick still smell like this wheeny ass nigga's baby mama's pussy! I'm in a great mood!" I pointed right at that nigga, so the crowd could laugh at him.

He started trying to get past his niggas, so he could attack me and that's when Jersey Joe threw a cup of liquor in his face, then it was on! They all started bum rushing the stage, and that's when it got real. I threw the microphone as hard as I could right at Butta's face. It hit his bitch ass dead in the eye. He yelled something and fell back holding his face. Next thing I knew I was squaring up with Pressha throwing those thangs. We were both throwing haymakers tryna' take each other's head off. He caught me with a stiff jab right in the eye, backing me up a lil bit.

"Yeah, nigga, talk that slob shit now!" he taunted while squaring back up.

"You know what's up, nigga, fuck crabs!" I shot back then rushed in swinging.

We were exchanging punches when all of a sudden, I felt the side of my head crash in and I went flying at the same time. Soon as I hit the ground, I got to my hands and knees tryna get back on my feet, but those niggas were on me! One of them pussies punched me in the jaw while the other kicked me in the side. I couldn't do nothing but cover up and hope one of my niggas seen me getting stomped out.

I don't know how long those niggas were on me, but it felt like an eternity, but then things drastically changed.

Boom! Boom! Boom! Boom! Boom!

The gun shots started, and I remember hearing one of the niggas kicking me, scream out like a bitch. All I heard was mass screaming and people running. The blows stopped raining on my body and I jumped up, trying to see what was going on. I saw Tamia waving my pistol from side to side keeping everybody away from me and making niggas jump off the stage. I saw Pressha helping a nigga that was shot in the leg run through the crowd. I ran over to Tamia and grabbed the heat and got to busting into the crowd.

Boom! Boom! Boom! Boom! Boom! Boom!

I didn't give a fuck who got hit! Gutta Squad niggas, my niggas or innocent bystanders! I had just got whooped on and my pride was fucked up.

Boom! Boom! Boom! Boom!

"O, come on nigga!" Bobbie grabbed my shoulder, yelling at me.

I picked my mask up off the floor, grabbed Tamia and broke back stage. Burnside was fighting with two rent a cops in the hallway. Those faggots were really tryna' arrest my nigga or something'. I smacked one of them niggas in the back of the head with the heat, dropping his bitch ass. I pointed it at the other one, freezing him up instantly. Soon as his hands went in the air, Burnside snuffed him and laid 'em out.

"Come on, blood, we gotta get to the guns!" Bobbie yelled at Burnside when he started kicking the guard.

We made it outside and all I saw was people running everywhere tryna' get to safety. I didn't know where my niggas was at, but I assumed they were making their way to the cars. So, I headed that way with the pistol gripped tightly.

Boc! Boc! Boc! Boc! Boca! Boc! Boca! Boca! Boca! Boca! Boc! Boc!

"Oh shit, them niggas is bustin'!" Bobbie yelled, as we got low from the shots.

They were coming from around the corner at the parking lot. I had felt it in my gut that it wasn't my niggas doing the shooting.

"Head straight for the car when you see that it's safe," I told Tamia, then sprinted towards the action.

Boc! Boc! Boc! Booya! Booya! Bloc! Bloc!

The shots started up again soon as I started running. When I finally got to the action, I saw a bunch of niggas running around cars shooting at each other. It was some real life wild, wild, west shit going on for real.

Boc! Boc!

I saw Gotti get hit in the side as he was ducking around a car. Next thing I knew, I was running after the gun man before he could close in on my relative.

Boom! Boom! Boom!

I got loose hitting the nigga somewhere in the back. He spun around with his gun aimed at me.

Boom! Boom!

The bullets hit 'em making him fly against the car dropping his gun. He slid down holding his stomach as I closed in.

"Wait –"

Boom! Boom! Boom! Boom!

I finished him off before he could finish begging for his life. I crushed that nigga, then looked at how he died in that awkward position. The last thing he saw was a nigga standing over him with a Michael Myers mask on, scary.

Boc! Boc! Blaat! Blaat! Boc! Boom! Boom! Boom!

I got low, as niggas started shooting again trying to find Gotti.

"Bro, where you at?" I called out to him.

"Over here, aghh shit!" he called out.

I found him crouching behind a car with his gun in his hand looking like he was fighting death.

"Where Joe and them niggas at?" I asked.

"Somewhere shootin' it out. Joe took one to the leg, but he was still up serving those niggas. Most of those crabs made it to their cars first, so they had the drop on us. Shit ain't lookin' good blood. Niggas hit me in the back."

"I know, but I crushed his bitch ass," I said, then pulled my phone out to call Tamia.

"Yo, come get me now. I got Gotti with me and he's hit I'ma stand in the lot till you find me. Hurry up!" I yelled at her.

The sirens could be heard now, the boys were on the way! A few gun shots could still be heard in the distance but not that many. Niggas knew it was time to go. Tamia pulled up right on time and helped Gotti get in, then we sped to the hospital.

Chapter 6
May 6th 5:00 a.m.

After we rushed Gotti to the hospital, we had to leave that nigga there and blow that joint immediately. Shit, I didn't even get out the car, that's how serious it was. I couldn't take the chance of the police kidnapping me or none of that funny shit. Soon as we left there, I had Tamia take me to the bridge, so I could toss the burner in the Willamette River, then we went straight to the condo which was only ten minutes away.

I changed clothes, made a few calls, grabbed my .38 snub nose and got back to the hospital to check on my niggas. The whole time in the car all Tamia wanted to talk about was how she had shot somebody for me, and she wasn't crying and complaining. No, she was taking and sounding like Burnside or one of those niggas! She was really hyped up and starting to think she was Giselle Deblanco 'cause she popped a crab in the leg or wherever, but I couldn't rain on my bitch's parade. So, I just let her feel herself, plus she did low-key save a nigga.

"What's it lookin' like?" I asked Burnside, as I walked up on the group.

Everybody was pacing around, or either talking to each other, or on their cell phones. The only person that was sitting down, was Joy. Actually, she was the only person that wasn't family that was even there.

"Shit, Joe, gucci. Just a lil' leg shot. I think he got hit around the ankle or some weak shit like that. Gotti shit went in and out. We just waiting on the doctors."

"You know I had to body one of those niggas. I don't even know who he was," I whispered.

"Yeah, I figured that. The nigga name was Freeze, he was one of their niggas. They been shouting him out on Facebook all night. Oh, they been putting MK, Mob Killa, after every post too." He shook his head at the last part.

"They still dry snitchin' on their blood, real talk. That shit be having me hot! Now they wanna act like the fuck boy was Tupac or summin', typical Portland shit," I spat.

That was some real shit though, on my mama. Every time somebody got killed in Portland, the whole town went crazy on Facebook and Instagram. Everybody was the new Tupac when they got killed, the shit was out of hand. Then, to make matters worse, the females stayed talking the most shit. Right then they were on their M-K trip. *We'll see what they say when they bump into us.* I ran a hand downmy face.

"Bro, did you see how I popped that nigga? Y'all gone have to start paying me for this shit, for real," Tamia jumped in, talking to Burnside.

He smiled at her. "Yeah, sis, I seen you put that work in. That nigga's name is Herbo, by the way." He feed her ego.

"Niggas wanna push real bitches to the side so they can play house with a square bitch. Where they do that at? I done had niggas run in my house. I done shot a nigga, and hold dope with the money, what more can I do? What you think, Burnside? Am I wifey material? Am I not a real bitch?" she posed.

"Shit, I'll wife you if he won't," Bobbie decided to add fuel to the fire.

"I'ma think about it," she shot back.

She wasn't about to get a rise out of me. My mind was way too strong for that. I'd never deny that Tamia was a real bitch, but she knew what she signed up for. I was with Olay when we met so she could protest all she wanted. It wasn't about to change nothing. If me and Olay was to break up, then she was next in line, period. She knew the rules.

Joe came hopping out on crutches a couple minutes later, looking mad at the world. Falon rushed over to hug him as soon as he walked into the waiting room and Joy was only a few steps behind.

"That hug looked like they were more than family to me. I think yo bitch feeling Jersey," I told Bobbie trying to see where his head was at.

Steady Mobbin'

"Nigga, we can 'G' that bitch far as I'm concerned, blood. We been rockin' and shit but it ain't like that, but ain't either one of them said nothin' bout fuckin' around. So, it must not be that serious, but fuck all that, blood, we got more important shit to discuss." He looked irritated that we were even having that discussion.

We all rushed the doctor at the same time.

"What about Devon Anderson?" I asked holding my breath.

"Mr. Anderson is heavily sedated right now, but he'll be just fine. The bullet went in and out very clean without hitting any arteries. He will be sore for a while, but nothing permanent," the middle-aged white doctor informed us.

"When can we see him, doc?" I asked.

"Possibly later on in the evening. He needs his rest right now." He answered a few more questions, then disappeared back through the doors.

"Yo, son, I'm killin' one of those crabs tonight!" Joe spat with a voice full of venom.

I knew he was dead serious, but I couldn't let him go out like that.

"Not until you get off those crutches, my nigga, give it a few weeks," I tried to reason with him.

"I don't give a fuck about no crutches, son. They don't affect my aim!" he spat.

"Here come the pigs," one of the homies blurted out before I could respond.

Everybody got to looking around nervous and like they were ready to run for it. Shit, most the niggas that were there had just been in that shoot out and probably still had those guns on them. Thank God, I had Tamia put mine in her purse before we came in.

"Y'all think I'll look good in a mug shot?" Tamia said, getting a few laughs.

She was taking that Giselle shit way too far. We watched the two-house nigga detectives make their way towards us. I hated those faggots to death and the whole rest of their gang task force team. I could never understand what made Blacks wanna be pigs or prosecutors. That shit blew my mind!

"What's up with the Mob Life?" Detective Freeman asked us like he was a real nigga or something.

"Never heard of no such thing," I answered.

"That's funny, O-Dawg, because you're the leader of it," Detective Rogers spoke up. That house nigga had the audacity to have dreadlocks.

"What the fuck you porch monkeys want? Can't you see we're grieving right now?" I said almost losing my anger. I really hated those punks.

They looked at each other, then Detective Freeman pulled his handcuffs out.

"We have probable cause to arrest you for murder," he told me. So, I turned around, so he could do his job.

I looked at Tamia. "Stay calm and don't get arrested. Call my lawyer and tell him what just happened," I stated real calm, but I was a nervous wreck inside.

"Okay, daddy, I will." She was trying not to cry and flip out. I could tell.

"Nigga, fuck one time!" Burnside yelled out, getting everybody hyped up.

"Uncle Tom ass nigga!" Bobbie yelled next.

"You punks keep talkin' and I'll arrest all your black asses," Detective Rogers yelled, then pulled his gun out. He sounded like a cracka, so proper and shit.

"Yeah, right, bitch ass nigga. You ain't gone do nothing! Don't pull no gun unless you ready to use it!" Trell got turnt up.

I knew it was time to defuse that shit cause all it took was for a few hot tempers and next thing we in a shootout. That was one we couldn't win.

"Fall back, they just fuckin' wit a real nigga. I'll be out this week. Don't fall for their lil mind games," I calmed my hittaz down. They got to pulling out their phones recording me getting escorted out. All I kept thinking was my pussy rate was really about to go up now.

76

Steady Mobbin'

Once we got to the interrogation room, I just sat there staring at those pussies with a look of defiance. The whole ride over, they just kept repeating how they had finally got my ass. They sounded real confident in the car and at first, I was a lil spooked, but after sitting in that room for ten minutes, it became clear they ain't have shit!

"So, you're saying you didn't kill Freeze?" Freeman asked again.

"I don't know no Freeze or whatever you said his real name was, and for the record I've never killed anybody in my life. We have summin' in common." I added that last line to get under their skin.

"Hmph! I doubt that," he replied, with a stupid ass look on his face.

"So, you never had a forty-five either?" he had the nerve to ask me.

"Never had one in my life," I answered quickly.

"Well, that's strange, because we have an eye witness who saw you with one. You can't just pull guns out and pass it without somebody seeing you," he said it with a cocky smirk on his face.

At that moment I knew he wasn't lying. I could see it all in his eyes, but he had just fucked up and he didn't even know it. Only two people saw me pull it out and I only did it that one time. Once he said I passed it, that sealed their caskets. Detective Rogers pulled some pictures out and laid them on the table, then went back to the corner to finish playing the bad cop role, just staring at me.

I picked them up, looked at them nonchalantly and flicked them on the table, one by one. The pictures were of the nigga I killed earlier, all different views. I felt not the slightest touch of remorse, fuck that nigga. I shrugged my shoulders, then said, "Looks dead to me." I sounded bored to death.

"Admiring your dirty work?" Freeman grinned, like he had me while trying to read me.

Marcellus Allen

"We already can place the murder weapon in your hand and I'll bet my ass we'll have a shit load more of witnesses by next week. So, just save yourself the trouble and tell us how it went down and if you really wanna save yourself. Well, we can go down that road too," he propositioned.

I started rubbing my chin like I was in deep thought, then I looked at both of them. "When you put it like that, somethin' did just cross my mind." Freeman leaned closer and Rogers actually walked over.

"I was watching that movie Django the other day and y'all remember that house nigga, that Samuel Jackson played? Both you bitches are worse than him! I know when y'all seen that movie y'all said to each other, man, he wasn't going hard enough! I want my lawyer! Get y'all race trading asses out my face and go find ya witnesses!" I yelled, then found a spot on the wall and stared at it.

"We'll see how much shit you're talking when we stick that needle in your arm!" one of them yelled, then they got the fuck out my face.

I was never worried about getting charged as I sat there. They had nothing but a snitch that saw me pass a gun. They weren't even sure if it was the same gun. The only thing that was on my mind was killing that snitch and getting it done ASAP. I was tryna' figure out in my head who had the motivation to do it. The nigga or the bitch? My lawyer had walked in as I was visualizing myself killing that nigga!

"You ready to go or do you wanna move in?" my lawyer asked with a smirk on his face.

There was no need to respond. I jumped up and broke out that room. I was determined to do whatever necessary to never get put in there again.

I was back home after hours of being kidnapped at that dumb ass precinct. From the moment I walked out those doors, somebody was complaining, giving me a damn headache! First it was Tamia with her whining and complaining. The whole car ride to her condo she kept saying how I didn't appreciate her or what she does for me. She was mad that I wasn't staying over to dick her down and I said I was going straight to my house. In her mind that meant I was rushing home to play house with Olay. Which meant I didn't really love her and all the other bullshit she was saying.

Then I get home expecting to find peace, but Olay started complaining as soon as I walk through the door! She had twenty-one questions for a nigga straight off the rip. *'Why didn't I call her?' 'Did you kill him?' 'Who picked you up?' 'Aren't you tired of this shit?'* Blah, blah, blah!

I picked my son up off the floor and headed to the basement leaving her ass up there complaining to herself. Then Spike called, and I had to hear his shit and all the lecturing he was doing. I was about to cuss his ass out when he basically demanded that I come to Atlanta, but then I got an idea. I hung up and played with my son while I waited for Bobbie to come through.

"What's brackin', nigga?" Bobbie came rushing down the stairs about an hour later.

"Shit, tryna' put it together. Why you look like you flew down here?" I asked while we shook up.

"To get away from his crazy ass mama," he said, then pointed at my son.

"What's good, lil nigga?" He dapped my son up.

My son nodded his head.

"Sup, nigga!" he shouted trying to sound all hard. That shit was comical.

"You better quit yelling before ya mama hear yo bad ass. Matter fact, go tell her to make you some food or summin'. Me and uncle gotta talk," I said, then waited until he was gone.

I looked my nigga up and down and could see the stress all over his face. He was a gangsta though, so I wasn't too much worried about him.

"You look like you ain't been to sleep," I told him.

"Shit, I haven't. I been at the hospital, then I had to hit the streets and check out a few problems. It's been hella shootings since last night. So, I had to tighten some of the spots up."

"Somebody snitched on me and I narrowed it down to two people. They tryna' build a case on me." All that other shit he was talking was irrelevant to me at that time. That was everyday shit, but being questioned for murder wasn't.

"What you mean they got a snitch! Who is it?" he jumped off the couch, yelling.

"I don't know the nigga name, but I know who does. Long story short, when I put the smack inside Tamia's purse, this weak ass rap nigga and his bitch saw me. The one I took the weed from and had Trell take his bitch. That weak ass nigga," I vented.

"We on that nigga tonight! I'ma make a few calls and get his name." He pulled out his phone getting ready to call, when I stopped him.

"Bobbie, we got the bitch," I stated matter factly.

He smirked, "Duh, what am I thinking? Aight, I'ma kill both of them, don't trip."

That was one of the reasons why I loved that nigga to death, his loyalty. There wasn't nothing he wouldn't do for the niggas he broke bread with. He didn't care about the consequences or none of that. If we needed him, he was there, period.

"Naw, that's gone be too hot. You starting to act like Burnside now." We both started laughing at that shit. Nobody was hot as Burnside, not even Joe.

"I'm bout' to slide to Atlanta tomorrow for a few weeks. Do it while I'm away. Have Trell finesse the situation for the info, then handle it. Then we'll see how the pigs respond when he gets smacked. If they're still cocky, then we'll hit the bitch."

He nodded in agreement. I could see the look of murder in his eyes.

Chapter 7
May 7th

"Blood, I seen so many thick ass bitches since I landed here thirty minutes ago! It must be summin' in the water," I announced to Spike, as we drove away from the airport.

I had just landed in the 'A' and it was already poppin'! All I seen was ass from the moment the plane landed.

"Yeah, all the bitches are thick down here in the South, so get used to it. Nigga, where ya bags at?" he replied in his deep ass voice. It was always funny to me how that nigga had the deepest voice but was damn near albino.

"C'mon, blood, this is me. I ain't with all that pushing luggage and shit. I'm too much of a real nigga for that. Take me to Lennox Mall. That's the one everybody be rapping about, right?" I said with pure arrogance.

He looked me up and down, then said, "What you wearing all that jewelry for, nigga? You going to a music video or summin'? You look like a walking lick."

I looked at myself, then shrugged like I could care less. I was heavy on the ice for a reason, cause I was in Atlanta! I had on my customized 'M' piece hanging off my neck plus the two Jesus pieces I always rocked. Iced out Rolex on the left wrist, with the canary yellow bracelet on the other. Then I topped it off with the diamond earring, and the pinky ring.

Yeah, I was on one that day with over $100,000 in diamonds, fuck whoever didn't like it.

"I wish one of these niggas would reach for my chain. That'll be the last one they ever reach for," I was still being arrogant.

He shook his head in frustration. "Nigga, this ain't Portland, blood. These niggas live off rolling down here," he said not hiding his irritation.

"Then they gone be dying off of it fuckin' with me. I'll show these niggas how to really gang bang! Matter fact, did you bring me that thang?" I wasn't tryna' hear what he was talking about.

He opened the glove box, then tossed a pistol on my lap. Now we were making progress. I examined it, a P89 Ruger, then took the clip out, fifteen shot magazine double. I cocked it back putting one in the head, then tucked it on my waist.

It took me a couple hours to drop a few bands at the mall, then we shook to the studio cause Spike had some sessions lined up. At first, I wasn't feeling it, thinking I was gone be on the couch while he worked with somebody else. Whatever negativity I had felt at first immediately went away as soon as we stepped inside the studio. When I say it was live, I mean that shit from the heart. The first thing I saw was two thick ass broads trying to out twerk each other! They weren't lying when they say they turn up in the 'A', the hype was real.

It was five young niggas in there, and all of them had dreads for some reason. I checked them out ASAP and could tell none of them was a threat. Then I started focusing on all the bitches in there. It was at least fifteen of them. Everybody was vibing to the song that was blasting. It had major 808 but the lyrics were trash, in my opinion   .

They had everything in there, from weed to drank to lean and even some pills in a bowl. All eyes went on us soon as we stepped in the room which was what I was accustomed to anyways.

I'm glad I wore all my ice was the first thought that came to mind when I watched all the broads size me up.

"You like this shit, huh?" Spike said, with a smirk on his face.

"Hell yeah, nigga. It's poppin' in here, on me!" I shot back.

"This shit gets old. It's always like this at every studio that I go to. Welcome to the 'A." Heactually sounded irritated.

"Yo, non-stop, what's good, nigga?" yelled the nigga sitting down at the computer yelled.

"Shit, let's knock this track out," Spike responded. He looked at me. "That's raw, he the one I'm working with. He a good nigga."

Steady Mobbin'

We walked over, and Spike introduced me to the Raw and all his lil sidekicks. I shook everybody up, but my mind kept going back to Spike warning me about cats down here loving to rob. The way those niggas was looking at my jewelry had me feeling some type of way. I wasn't worried though, that pistol was right on my hip.

'Nigga took my chain, yeah muthafuckin' right/nigga better off saying he took my life.' Those Jeezy lyrics popped in my head at that moment, maybe since we were in the 'A'.

"Damn, who is you?" a light skinned chick with a fat ass asked me. Women in Atlanta were real bold. I found that out earlier that day at the mall.

"My name O-Dawg. Why, what's up?" I shot back with a smile.

"Nothing, you! Where you from?"

"How you know I ain't from here?"

"Cause how you dress, that's how," she explained.

"What you mean how I dress?" I looked myself up and down. I knew I was dipped in all that designer shit.

"No, not like that. You dress real nice, just different, that's all," she said.

"I'm from Portland. It's in Oregon." I broke it down to her, cause every girl I met at the mall didn't even know where Portland was. That shit was hella crazy to me and it low-key pissed me off.

"They don't dress like that in Portland," she declared while staring me up and down hungrily.

"They don't dress like me anywhere," I replied full of arrogance and slightly irritated, "but fuck all that, what's yo name and what the business is?" I got straight to the point.

"My name is Tisha," she said, giving me a sexy smile.

"Yo, O, come over here real quick," Spike called me over, messing up the flow.

I walked over to him and Raw at the engineering board.

"What's Mobbin', nigga? You fuckin' up my game," I let it be known.

"Blood, I be fuckin' her home girl all the time. We'll get them to swing by tonight, don't trip," Spike said, then looked over to the group of girls that was eyeing us.

"Anyways, you got that song you said you finished on the plane?"

"Yeah, you talkin' bout that 'Murder was the Case'? I got it wrote in my phone. Why, what's the move?"

"When I'm done with his joint, we gone start working on yours. At least knock the first verse out. I got an idea for a sample we can start the song off with."

"Aight, I'ma be ready," I replied, then looked at Raw. "Good lookin' out, nigga, on letting me record here," I said.

"You good, shawty. Real niggas gotta look out for each other. Plus, Non-Stop say you dat nigga. I'm tryna' hear summin' doe," Raw said in his southern while dapping me up. I only understood half of what the fuck he was saying.

I left those niggas and made my way to the couches where it was poppin' at. They had the weed in rotation, plus I seen a couple broads eyeing me over there since I walked in.

"Sup wit it, kinfolk? You tryna' hit dis bitch?" one of the dread heads I met earlier passed me the blunt.

"Yeah, let me hit it a few times, blood." I hit it, then passed it to the next person.

I noticed a thick ass chocolate broad sitting next to me all in my mouth and eyeing me. I checked her out from head to toe and definitely loved what I saw. She had big titties and thunder thighs, so I just knew that ass was fat. I almost told her to stand up.

"What's up with it? My name O-Dawg. I see you checking me out and I hope you like what you see cause I definitely like what I see," I said getting ready to get my mack on.

She smiled, "You talk so proper. It's cute though," she answered, then boldly looked me up and down like she was about to eat me or something.

"I been hearing that all day but it still don't make sense to me. I just talk normal," I said.

84

Steady Mobbin'

Everybody in the South said we talk proper on the West Coast, but that shit sounded dumb to me. I loved the South, but I couldn't understand half the shit they say, real talk.

"It means you talk White, like you White or summin,'" she had the audacity to say.

That shit pissed me off, comparing me to White people like I ain't a real nigga or summin', but before I could respond to her, the blunt came back my way and that saved her ass. I took a few long pulls, then passed it.

"Aye, big dawg, so you nice on da mic?" another one of those dread niggas asked me.

"Yeah, I fucks with it, you'll see in a minute."

I was still feeling some type of way about all that slick shit they had said. Acting like Portland niggas don't dress like I do, I talk White and all the other bullshit they said. I told myself not to take it personal. They just ain't never been around Portland niggas.

I ended up getting the chocolate broad's number and choppin' it up with those niggas for another hour until Spike called me over to listen to the beat he had for me. I knew that shit was the one from the moment it leaked through the speakers.

It had a dope ass Scarface sample to start it off. It was the scene from the movie when they set Tony up counting all that money, then he told them how good his lawyer was and to dress warm. It was heavy!

"Once you hear those gun shots, that's when you start yo verse. Ain't no hook, the sample just replays after each verse," he explained to me.

I stood there rapping real low to myself tryna' make sure I was riding the beat right. I felt myself getting pumped up. I got the feeling that all the greats get right before they do something great.

"You ready, dawg? Let us hear dat West Coast fiyah," Raw said.

He seemed genuine, he wasn't on no competitive shit. He really wanted to see if I had it. I didn't even reply, wasn't nothing to say. I just walked in the booth still tryna' get the pattern down right. I told Spike give me two minutes to get my shit down pat. After I knew I had it down, I stepped up to the mic.

"Turn me up in the headphones," I told him, then kept reciting my bars off of my phone.

"Hear it come," Spike said, then the lights got dim. Just how I liked it.

I looked around and everybody was fully focused on me. They all wanted to see if my bars would match my confidence, I could tell. The nigga that asked could I rap, was staring the hardest while he was hitting the weed.

I heard the gunshots, and went in.

Picked me up for a body few hours after they shot Gotti/my lawyer a beast so his fee is a new Maserati/I'ma get killed probably, tell mama I'm sorry/but I'ma get rich till they blame it on Illuminati/Death threats everyday got me clutchin/ shot Joe, it's nothin', he taking field trips on his crutches/Michael Myers mask like it's Halloween/catch a body for the team, MAC 90 with the beam/ya main shooter a fien' tell 'em to snort summin'/I put 20 grand on ya head now you worth summin'/at ya homie grave-site smiling at his tombstone/got the devil in me bitch nigga shouldn't of moved wrong/my mama ask how I sleep wit these bodies on my conscience/I told her like a baby, and does that make me a monster?/snitch nigga wanna put a murder case on me/I told Bobbie put the murder victim face on 'em.

After I finished the first verse I got to get a good breather in case that sample was kinda long. Then I knocked the second verse out and it was a wrap. When I stepped out the booth all the niggas were nodding at me and pounding their chests showing me mad love. The women still had those looks of lust in their eyes, but now I could really see the thirst. Raw dapped me up, and then he turned to Spike.

"You need to get dis nigga poppin' down here, dawg, like fo'real fo'real. On Blood, he fiyah."

Steady Mobbin'

His compliment meant something to me for some reason. I guess cause he was really in the industry and had a name for himself.

"I appreciate that, fam. Aye, you a damu?" I asked cause he said blood, but I didn't know if that was just an Atlanta word or what.

"Hell yeah, dawg. We push that five in dis bitch, sex, money, murder. Why, what's poppin', Slime?" he asked while he got to throwing all types of shit up. Luckily, I done watched enough of those East Coast blood documents to understand what the hell he was asking.

"I'ma Damu, but I'm not poppin' or under the five like y'all niggas is. We don't do that on the West Coast, contrary to popular belief, but I fuckz with y'all though. I'm from the Mob Life, Denver Lane gang though, feel me?" I let it be known, then I threw the Mob up followed by the 'L' for Lanes.

"Yo Slime over here a West Coast homie. Y'all niggas come over here and show respect, dawg," Raw announced.

They hopped up like a nigga was the president or something. They tried shaking me up with some long ass East Coast/South blood shake I seen on Gangland or somewhere. When that didn't work out, I just showed them the basic shake we did on the West and left it at that. Them niggas got to asking hella questions about California and Portland but it was all gucci in my books. They had never been around a real West Coast blood, so it was understandable. I got those niggas lines and we agreed on linking up before I left. Shit, they even told me if I everyl needed them to come to Portland and kill summin', to just let them know.

Next Day

"Wake up, nigga, we got shit to do," Spike said while pounding on the door.

"I'm up! Hold on, blood!" I yelled out, mad that he woke me up.

Tisha started moving around under the covers too, probably mad she got woke up. I slapped her on the ass to make sure she was fully awake.

"C'mon, it's time to get up," I told her.

"Ouch, boy, that hurt!" she yelled from under the cover.

"You wasn't saying that last night," I teased her.

That night was definitely something to remember cause she was a freak for real. As soon as we walked in the room, she straight attacked me. I'm talking about threw me against the wall and snatched my clothes off within seconds. Talkin' bout she always wanted to fuck a West Coast nigga. She let me put it in all three holes, swallowed my nut and everything in between.

"You wasn't, either." She came from under the covers with a smile on her face. She started stroking my meat while she waited for me to say something.

"What you about to do with that?" I asked.

Whatever you want."

"I love you South bitches, on the Mob," I told her, then pulled the covers off me, so she could get a good look at it.

She smiled, then put it in her mouth and went to work. I grabbed my phone off the dresser and started recording it. When she saw the phone, that's when she really went in, deep throating and all. I guess she wanted a nigga to really remember her and I definitely would. After another ten minutes of that, I was ready to bust my nut and that's exactly what I did.

"Aghh! Shit!" I moaned out while pushing her head down far as it would go.

After I got through with her, I made my way to Spike's home studio where he was hard at work on a new beat. He looked at me real quick, then got back on his machine. I just stood there watching him perfect his craft, noticing how focused he was. My nigga took his shit serious. After another twenty minutes, he finally turned the music down and looked at me.

"I'ma mix and master yo shit later on. Have it sounding real professional," he assured me.

Steady Mobbin'

"Aight, what's the plan for today? You came to the door like we had summin' to do right now," I replied.

"Naw, it was just time for them hos to get out my shit. They know the drill. You can sit down and start writing to these beats though."

"Man, blood, you should have had those bitches cook breakfast before you kicked them out," I complained.

"What, you hungry or summin'?"

"Hell yeah, I'm hungry, nigga. What type of shit is you on?" He started laughing.

"Aight get dressed, I'ma take you to Gladys Knight's Chicken and Waffles."

"I don't eat my waffles with no damn chicken, nigga."

"Blood, just get dressed so we can eat and hurry up and get back."

When I hopped in the car, Spike looked at me and shook his head before pulling off.

"What you shaking yo head for, nigga?" I asked already knowing the answer.

"You just had to wear all that jewelry. What you gone do? Stunt on breakfast?" he asked, being sarcastic.

"Nigga, I'ma wear all my jewels in my casket, so why not to breakfast? This what I do, blood, and you know that."

For the rest of the ride, I talked on my phone letting everybody know what I wanted and how I wanted it done. Bobbie told me that they had a line on the snitch nigga and it was gone be handled real soon. He also let me know that Jersey Joe was on some bullshit and was acting like what he said didn't matter.

He told me how he felt that Joe had some type of animosity towards him for no reason. He really wasn't feeling how Joe kept calling him 'Boss' every time he gave a directive or what not. I told him not to trip, that those meds probably just had him trippin', but truth be told, I had my own suspicions that I was gonna look into.

Marcellus Allen

When we stepped into Gladys Knights, it was packed with beautiful sistas and business niggas rockin slacks and shit. There were some people dressed casual too but nobody lookin' like me. That didn't bother me one bit though. I liked standing out. I was a standout type of nigga. A sexy, petite waitress showed us to our table and I couldn't help myself.

"You're beautiful," I told her while staring dead in her eyes. She smiled, "Thank you."

"Can I know your name?"

"Lashay," she said pointing at her name tag still smiling.

"I know it's probably against the rules for you to give me your number, so I'ma write my info on the receipt and hopefully you use it," I told her.

She smiled again, then walked off. I watched her lil' ass jiggle until she was out of sight. That's when I noticed all the pictures on the walls with famous people eating in the restaurant. I liked that spot before I even tasted the food, plus all the waitresses were sexy and they all had their eyes on me, real talk.

"I love Atlanta, blood," I confessed to Spike.

"Then move down here and stop playing. We need to work on getting you poppin' down here in the strip clubs, that's how it works. I'm telling you, you'll blow up in no time. Soon as I'm done finishing these beats for the Migos, we can get yo shit done," he said.

"By the time you're done with them, I should be done with those pussies in Portland." My blood started boiling from just thinking about them niggas.

He sighed, then shook his head, "I don't know!"

"Come on, blood, don't even start with that shit." I cut him off before I picked the menu up. "I'ma street nigga that just happens to rap. If this music shit works out, then cool', but I'm not about to stop my hustle just to find out," I let him know before he could start that 'get out the streets' lecturing shit.

We chopped it up about the music industry in general and how everything works for about an hour before it was time to leave. I could tell he wanted to bring up that shit again, but he knew better. He could talk until his face turned blue, and I still wasn't gone change my mind. I felt like I was on top of the world, so why would I throw that away for a pipe dream? Naw, I was gone keep getting money and dropping mixtapes like I had been doing. If I blew up, then we good, if not, I was gone get a million out the streets.

Marcellus Allen

Chapter 8
May 23rd

I walked off the plane a few weeks later with a whole lot on my mind. I loved Atlanta, I couldn't lie, but I had a whole lot of shit to set straight in my own city. The city that I ran. So much had happened in the few I was gone, some good, some bad. But the realest is back now, I thought to myself as I walked out of the PDX with the sun glaring in my eyes. I'm back on my North-East shit, I said to myself while I looked around for Olay.

"Hey scumbag, you want a ride?" Detective Rogers said, as him and his partner hopped out of an unmarked.

"Black people don't say scumbag. What you house niggas want?" I shot back, still looking for my bitch's Range Rover.

"We just wanted to welcome you back to the war zone you created. Where's your bags?"

"Rich niggas don't do bags. I don't have a salary or save for a pension either. I'm straight cash, homie. Now, what the fuck you pigs want? I don't know where Django at."

"Real funny, shit head," Detective Freeman growled as he got in my face. "We know you had our witness killed. I just wanted to let you know that now it's personal," he threatened me.

"I don't know what you're talkin' about," I lied, "and your breath smells like swine, but I'm glad you're taking shit personal now, I like it like that," I taunted him.

Before his bitch ass could respond, my cell phone rung in my pocket. I was about to reach for it, but then remembered I was dealing with Portland gang task. I wasn't going out like that, plus, I knew by the ringtone it was Olay calling.

"Hey partner, be careful that he doesn't reach for a weapon," Detective Rogers said with an evil grin on his face.

I saw Olay parked at the curb. "I'll see you house niggas later, my bitch is here," I said, then walked off on those pigs. Freeman bumped into me tryna' get a reaction but that wasn't about to happen.

Marcellus Allen

I jumped in the Rover and gave wifey a kiss, then looked at my son in the back seat. He was so focused on some movie he was watching that he didn't even notice me.

"Dada, you don't see me?" I said to him.

His eyes got wide when he saw me. "Daddy! Daddy!" he yelled spitting his pacifier out and kicking his feet.

"Hold on, dada, let me talk to mommy real quick," I said, then turned to Olay, "You look beautiful, baby."

"Thank you, baby," she said smiling.

I grabbed her thigh, then slowly ran my hand up her dress.

"Edible?" I asked.

"Then eat me," she responded while closing her legs on me.

"I plan on it," I smirked, then got to looking in the rearview mirror.

"Is gang task behind us?"

"I don't think so. That's who you were talking to?" She looked in the mirror and responded.

"Yeah, did you bring my gun?"

She sighed, "It's in the glove box, Marshawn, damn."

"A'ight, I'ma have you drop me off at the studio."

She damn near got whip lash how fast she turned her neck at me.

"Nigga, you ain't going to no fuckin' studio, so get that out your head right now. I already made reservations at Portland City Grill for tonight and we're not cancelling. You've been gone for weeks and the first thing you wanna do is go play with your friends?" She flashed on me.

I didn't even respond, cause it would have been pointless. My ass was going to Portland City Grill. My son threw his pacifier at me hitting the glove box instead.

"That's right, baby, hit daddy for me," Olay encouraged him.

"Pick me up, Daddy!" my son started yelling and kicking his feet out.

I lifted his lil bad ass out of his car seat and brought him up there with us.

94

"You throwing stuff at me huh?"

Then we got to play fighting like we were at the house or summin'.

"Mar Mar, get yo butt back in yo car seat before I whoop yo lil' ass," Olay said.

"Say shut up, mommy, before daddy get on you," I told him.

"I wish you would," she threatened, then mugged him.

When I seen he wasn't about to say nothing, I changed the subject. "Where he going, cause I know you ain't letting him rock with us tonight."

"He sho ain't. Falon coming over," she said.

That was good, because I definitely needed to holla at her sooner than later. I had planned on calling her that night but a face to face was even better.

I stood in the mirror fixing my Burberry button up and brushing my waves, I was on my fly shit. The place where we were going to eat had a strict dress code, so I had to get my grown man on. I loved dressing up anyways. Truth be told, I preferred to dress like that. I had on some black and brown snake skin Stacey Adams shoes, black slacks and a white Burberry button up with the pattern on the cuffs and neck line. I looked at myself again after fixing my collar. *Fly nigga.*

Olay walked in with Falon right behind her. I looked at them through the mirror and kept brushing my hair. So much had happened while I was gone that needed to be handled, but I was stuck dealing with Falon first and her messiness.

"Hey, bro, what you wanted to talk to me about?" Falon said while sitting down on my bed.

"About you acting like a fuckn' ho, let's start there," I grilled her, then turned to face her so she could see how serious I was.

"What, nigga? I'm not no ho and don't come at me like that." She sounded offended.

"Yeah, don't be talking to my sister like that, Marshawn. What the hell is wrong with you?" Olay jumped in.

I looked at Olay like she had two heads. "First off, you shut the fuck up and mind yo business. When it comes to this Mob shit, you stay silent. I wouldn't give a fuck if she was yo grandma. Now finish getting dressed before I change my mind and get to flippin' out," I checked her. I couldn't believe she had the audacity.

"Whatever!" she said, then went to the closet. She just wanted to have the last word.

"What are you talking about, O?" Falon played dumb.

I exhaled, "I'm talkin' about two of my closest niggas getting into it about petty shit when I know you're really the reason behind it. Nobody else knows, but I know, so don't sit here and play dumb with me," I grilled her.

She looked like she was about to deny it, but then I could see the guilt creep onto her face. It was all in her eyes. She knew what the fuck was going on.

"Bro, I'm not doing nothing but living my life and getting money. I ain't told that nigga to start trippin' over me," she half confessed.

She was so dumb, she didn't even realize how she had just told on herself. That let me know she knew exactly what I was talking about and she was fully aware of one of them trippin'. She probably thought the shit was a joke.

"Which one you talkin' about trippin' and don't lie to me, sis?" I asked, already knowing the answer.

She sucked her teeth, "Joe, he be on some possessive shit sometimes," she confessed.

"What he be saying?" I asked.

"How I need to stop fuckin' with Bobbie and just let him wife me. How Bobbie don't love me. How he does and when you move to do your music shit, that him and Burnside gone be runnin' shit. That Bobbie only got juice because he be on yo dick, but when you leave, how I'ma see who end up runnin' shit. Blah, blah, blah!" she said, and I knew she was telling the truth.

I didn't know how serious I should take what she was saying. I was pretty sure he said all of that, but niggas will say anything to knock a bitch. Joe knew Bobbie was certified, that's why I felt like it was just talk. Like he was just dirty macking, nothing more. I knew I was gone have to holla at him and see where his head was really at before shit got crazy.

"You're fuckin' two niggas in the same circle, Falon? You need to stop. You know how niggas get over pussy."

Olay jumped back in. "Hold up!"

"Olay, shut up," Falon started, but I cut her off.

"We not about to do all that," I spoke loud cutting that argument off short.

"I'm not about to tell you what to do with yo pussy, Falon, but I *am* gone tell you how you're going to do it. Either tell those niggas that you're fuckin' both of them, but it's not serious, or cut one off. I'm not gone let some pussy tear down my empire. I'll kill you before that happens. I love you, but I will kill you." I gave it to her raw. She didn't have anything to say, just sat there with her mouth open. So, I walked out.

When we got in the car Olay kept cutting her eyes at me while I was driving, but I didn't care. I just kept talking on the phone to all my niggas handling my business. I was in the middle of telling Bobbie what those house niggas did at the airport, when Olay punched me in the arm out of nowhere.

"Get off the phone, Marshawn!" She had reached her breaking point.

I hung up, "What you want, woman?" I asked.

"You can't just threaten to kill my lil' sister like that and you did it in front of me too," she whined.

I looked over at her and seen the look of concern on her face and decided not to flash on her, she was only being a woman.

"Baby, she's playing a dangerous game with some dangerous niggas," I explained to her.

"I know, daddy, but she's not gonna do it no more. I talked to her when you left. She knows what she's gotta do," she tried sweet talking me.

"Then we shouldn't have a problem, baby. Look, don't worry about it, I'm sure it's nothing. I just wanted to nip it in the bud that's all," I assured her.

"Would you really kill my only sister?" she asked after going silent for a few minutes.

"No, baby, I just wanted to scare her," I lied.

She leaned over and started kissing me. I pulled up to the gas station a few minutes later and told her to hand me her purse so I could grab the banger before I went in to pay for gas.

"Baby, you're doing way too much. Just go pay and hurry up so we don't end up late. You don't need no gun to do that. Where you gone tuck it at?" she complained.

Something told me to grab it anyways, but I didn't feel like wasting time with her. Plus, it would have been hard to conceal, and we were downtown Portland, the land of the rich. It was one small section where niggas sold dope but other than that, doing anything illegal was a no no. After I came out from paying for the gas, I noticed what looked like some niggas staring at me from inside a blue Benz. I shook it off as paranoia as I made my way back to the car.

I sat there for a minute tryna' process where I recognized that Benz from. Not too many niggas had a S550 in the town, especially blue.

"Baby, come on, what you waiting for?" Olay snapped me out of my zone.

Soon as we got to the red light, that same Benz pulled up right next to me. The window rolled down and we locked eyes for a split second. That's when I remembered whose Benz it was, Butta's, but the nigga that was staring was Pressha, his right-hand man. Soon as I saw the gun come out the window, I yelled for Olay to duck and smashed the pedal at the same time.

Boc! Boc! Boc! Boc! Boc! Boc! Boc!

I ducked down as I heard Olay yell and the glass raining down on me. I sped through the red light and so did they.

Boc! Boc! Boc! Boc! Boc!

98

I felt my arm go numb, that shit hurt. I was always heard when you get shot, that you don't feel it until later. Lie!

Boc! Boc! Boc!

Them niggas were really on me! I looked up real quick to see where I was going and that's when I saw a car shooting out in front of me. I tried hitting the breaks to lessen the impact that was inevitable. The last thing I remember was shielding Olay as the cars collided.

May 25th

I woke up two days later, in the hospital with a massive headache that felt like my head was splitting in half. When I was able to get my vision, the first thing I saw was Olay and Gotti staring down at me. Olay said, "Thank God!" She kissed me before she ran out the room to get the nurse.

"How many times they hit me, blood?" I wasted no time asking Gotti.

"Just twice. One in the arm and the other one hit ya shoulder. A third one grazed yo neck, but that don't count."

I looked over at my left arm in a sling, wrapped in bandages.

"Anytime I shed a drop of blood that shit counts, nigga," I declared. I felt myself heating up as I spoke those words.

"I know that's right, but just so you know, we've been fuckin' the city up over that shit. We got one of their main shooters too. Bobbie did," he whispered to me.

"What they hit me with?"

".45, they went straight through too," he answered.

"They tried to kill my wifey, blood. The gloves are off now," I spat. Just the thought of that caused the devil to run through me.

Gotti looked at me like he had something to say but didn't wanna say it. I thought it was a look of disagreement until I looked closer in his eyes.

"What aren't you telling me, blood?" I confronted him.

He exhaled deeply. "They grazed Olay on the head and the boys are charging her with the .40 that was in her purse, but it's only a misdemeanor since she ain't a felon," he spoke hella fast.

"Olay! Olay!" I yelled out, not giving a fuck what that nigga had to say anymore. I tried to get up, but he pushed me back down. "Olay!" I yelled again.

She finally walked in looking concerned.

"What's wrong, baby?" she asked while walking over to me.

"Let me see your head, Olay!"

"Baby, wait until," she began, but I cut her off.

"Let. Me. See. Your. Head!"

She leaned over and pushed her hair out the way about two inches above her temple. As soon as I saw those stitches I felt nothing but evil rushing through my veins. She stepped back and looked at me.

"The doctors said you probably saved me from more damage." She tried to make me feel better.

"Go tell the doctor I want out of here right now," I gritted, as I hurried up and wiped the tear that was forming in my eye. "Now it's really on, nigga! I'm killing the dog and the kids! Them niggas almost killed my baby mama, Gotti," I spat soon as she walked out.

"I know, bro."

Before I could go any further, the two house niggas walked in fuckin' up my mood even more. I really hated those niggas. They walked over wearing stupid ass smirks on their faces. Detective Rogers pulled out his notepad.

"Alright, let's get this out the way, Marshawn, because we know you're ready to spill the beans. So, who shot you and your pretty little girlfriend?"

"Mention her again and I promise I'ma kill you in due time," I spat, then tried to get up. Gotti pushed me back down.

"Just give us the names," Detective Freeman spoke up.

The doctor and the nurse came in followed by Olay. The doctor shined his light in my eyes and started asking me a thousand questions while the nurse was checking my wounds.

"I'm ready to leave, doc," I told him.

"I heard, but you still have a mild concussion. So, I want to keep you here another night. You should be ready by tomorrow. Just hang tight," he said.

I was getting ready to argue with him until Olay spoke up.

"I'll stay the night with you, baby. Just stay until tomorrow. You gotta get rid of your concussion, please!" she begged.

I was sore as a muthafucka and I could tell that whatever medicine they had me on was wearing off. Plus, I had that headache, I was in no shape to leave and I knew it. I needed some more morphine, but I wasn't taking nothing until those pigs left. They weren't about to have me answering questions while I was sedated. I knew too many niggas that tried to explain away their snitchin' on the medication. Maybe it was true, but I wasn't about to find out!

"Yo, doc? I'll stay, and I need some more morphine, but first, I need you to escort those two coops out of here. I already invoked my lawyer rights and I don't wanna be questioned under sedation."

"Sorry, detectives, but I'm going to have to ask you to leave," the doctor told them.

They looked frustrated and like they wanted to protest but decided not to. When they got close to the door I couldn't help but to rub it in.

"Rogers, the answer to y'all question is simple. Whoever y'all have to pick up off the ground. It's going to be a long summer and winter, so dress warm," I taunted, then they walked out.

After the doc hooked me up with that shot and left, I gave my attention to wifey.

"I'ma have my lawyer tell the DA that was my gun, baby," I let her know.

She shook her head, "No, Marshawn, you can go to prison and I can't. I got it, it's fine."

"No, baby, that's going to look bad for your golf career and we can't have that," I told her.

"That's one I'ma have to take then, because I'm not letting you go to prison," she defied me again.

I could tell she was dead serious and it made me love her even more. My heart was swelling with pride over how loyal my bitch was. *I know how to pick 'em,* I thought to myself at that moment. She talked all that square shit but when it came down to it, she was just as down as all the rest of the real hood bitches.

As much as I wanted to take her up on her offer, I couldn't. A real man doesn't let no harm come his woman's way. I was supposed to sacrifice for her, not the other way around, and I was about to make that clear.

"Not gone happen, Olay, bottom line. I'm sure my lawyer can get it thrown out for illegal search and seizure. They had no right going through your purse. Just let me take care of it, baby. I love you!" I told her.

"Oh, my baby!" I heard a woman yell and already knew who it was before looking at her.

My mother walked in carrying her Bible and sped over to me hugging me tight. I loved moms to death and it definitely made me feel better when she got to hugging me. When she let go, I could see the tears getting ready to fall down her face.

"I'm gucci, Mama," I assured her, then my medication kicked in, knocking me out.

Steady Mobbin'

Chapter 9
June 1st

It took me a week of staying in the house to finally feel good enough to leave that bitch. That whole week all I did was pop pain killers and record music. It did give me a lot of time to spend with my son that I usually wouldn't have had. Man, I was the talk of Facebook for a full week and they even blew me up on the news for a few days. They were talking about aspiring rapper gunned down, 'local rap star takes multiple bullets.' Shit, they made it seem like a real nigga was already dead.

One good thing that came out of that situation was that my I-tune sells were up, and my YouTube views were through the roof. I was dropping two-minute freestyles every day at one o'clock just to keep the buzz up. I had a few things planned for that day, so right after my freestyle was done, I started getting dressed.

I was going to throw on that fly shit, but changed my mind when I remembered what was on the agenda. So instead, I put on some grey Jordan sweats, red Jordan hoody and the red and black ones. I still had my arm in that dumb ass sling even though it didn't really hurt when I took it out, but the doctors said to keep it stable for a few more days and I didn't feel like hearing Olay's mouth.

My phone went off. I saw it was a text message from Burnside, telling me they were outside. So, I yelled upstairs for wifey to open the door.

Burnside and Bleed came walking down the stairs a few minutes later. My nigga, Bleed, had just got out the day before from doing a three-year bid. That was my first time seeing him since he spent his first day out tied up in the house with his baby mama. He was one of the most loyal niggas since grade school and I had never seen him switch it up.

He was dark skinned, about 5'10", and had braids that barely had any hang time.

103

"Man, blood, this house big as a muthafucka," Bleed said in his squeaky high-pitched voice.

"Wait til I cop the new one next year on them bitch ass niggas," I replied arrogantly then gave my nigga a 'G' hug.

"Olay still bad as a muthafucka with her lil' tight jiggly booty," he said with a smile, causing Burnside to start laughing.

"Don't make me fuck yo baby mama, nigga!" I shot back.

"Man, fuck that bitch, blood, she probably tried to fuck you while I was gone anyways," he said, then laughed at his own joke.

"I'm glad you home though, my nigga. Shit just got real." I changed topics.

"Yeah, I can see that." He nodded towards my arm, then sat down on my pool table. "When the fuck did Butta get so hard? He always been a bitch, on me," he added.

Burnside got off the couch. "That's gone take all day, I'm bout to go set that thang in motion," he said.

"Aight, we'll link up later," I replied, then shook him up.

"How shit get like this?" Bleed asked.

I didn't even know where to start to be honest. So much had happened between those years that I damn near forgot what the beef was all about. So many shootings, songs, and fights had happened, it was crazy, but really there was only one real answer to all the madness.

"They want the keys to the town and we holding them. You know it's always been a lil' friction between us, but when Burnside fucked Felicia, that's when it got heavy. We had to jump Half Dead, then shots got fired and it's been building up for years. They tried to off me like a month ago and it's been green light ever since," I broke it down to him.

He nodded his head. "It is what it is at this point, blood." He was loyal to a fault, so there was nothing else for him to say.

"Let's shake so we can go handle this business," I said, then headed up the stairs.

When we got outside, I popped the trunk to the new 2017 all black Camaro and threw the duffle bag full of money in it.

"This muthafucka still smell like you ain't never drove it," Bleed said after we jumped in.

"That's cause I just bought it a few weeks ago and I haven't." I had my arrogance turned all the way up as I sped off, dialing Tamia on my phone.

"Hello," she answered.

"I'll be at Gino's in a minute." I hung up without waiting for a reply.

She had been on her lil trip the whole time I was in Atlanta and she got even worse once I got back. She was hot she couldn't come see me in the hospital, cause Olay wouldn't leave my side and I wasn't about to rock that boat. Then the whole week I was in the house she was sending me hate text messages, talkin' about I was playing house. Something was really wrong with that broad.

"What the hell is Gino's?" Bleed asked me.

"The dealership we be getting our cars from. The Italian nigga be letting us cop under the table if we come with that bread," I explained.

"What you going there for when you just bought this one? You going hard," he replied.

"I'm bout to go cop some shit that's putting me on a whole 'nother level than these bitch ass niggas. This a nice ass ride, but this the type of shit you like. Muscle cars, old school and donks, that's yo shit. That's why I copped this bitch for you," I told him, then watched his face register what I had just told him.

"Blood, stop playin'. This me for real?" he asked still tryna' figure out if I was playing or not.

I opened the glove box and grabbed the title and insurance and tossed it on his lap. I rotated from driving to watching him sort through the paperwork with a smile on his face.

"Everything in yo baby mom name. What you thought I was gone have you out here lookin' like a mere mortal? Nigga, we on supreme status," I boasted.

"Good lookin', blood. I love you, my nigga. You already know I got you on whatever," he declared all emotional and shit.

Showing emotions wasn't something I was good at, especially with other niggas. I loved my niggas and they loved me. We all knew that, so we just kept it like that. Being in the streets made a nigga heart cold, so showing emotions was taboo. I turned up Kevin Gates *Neon Lights* and put the pedal to the metal. I wanted to see what that bitch could do before I handed the keys over.

When we pulled up to the lot, Tamia was already waiting with her homegirl and I could sense her attitude before I even parked. Soon as they recognized me, her homegirl hopped in her car and sped off. That was Tamia's way with being stuck with me. I wasn't trippin' cause we had a ritual every time I copped a whip.

"Damn blood, where your friend go?" Bleed complained.

"You don't want her, trust me. Come on, I got something for you," I told him as we headed to the trunk.

"I wanna fuck Tamia, she thick as a muthafucka, blood."

"She crazy as a muthafucka too. Lift that bag up for me, so I can grab it," I said.

"I'll just carry it for you, nigga," he said while lifting it. "Got damn, how much money in this bitch," he asked after putting it on his shoulder.

"Stop crying, nigga." I started laughing at him. "That other bag is yours, that's from all the homies," I pointed to a second bag in the trunk.

"Good lookin', blood. I'm bout to go shopping, on me. Yo, how much in this heavy ass bag!" he asked again as we made our way to the entrance where Tamia was waiting.

"One fifty, nigga."

"What the fuck you buying, a yacht?"

I just smirked. "You bout to see."

Tamia folded her arms and screwed her face up as we approached. She was looking for an argument and she wasn't about to get it.

"What you standing there with an attitude for?" I asked.

106

Steady Mobbin'

"Because I've been trying to spend time with you all week and you've been blowing me off, but soon as you need something, who's the first person you call?" she said with a major attitude.

"You look really pretty," I said, then slowly looked her up and down. She was wearing some stretch pants, a small shirt that stopped at her belly ring and had on some red heels. She even had her long hair let down. Just the way I liked it. She knew what she was doing.

"Tamia, this my bro Bleed. Bleed, this Tamia crazy ass," then I walked inside.

Gino speed walked over as soon as he saw me walk in that bitch. I had already called him earlier, but I guess it was something about seeing a duffle bag full of money that made a man put a pep in his step. I could see the dollar signs in his eyes as he stood in front of me.

"Mr. Anderson, how's my favorite client doing today?" he greeted with his hand out.

"Come to pick her up and drop this off," I replied, then motioned for Bleed to hand the bag over.

"Stephanie, take this to my office," he called his blonde assistant over, handing her the bag.

"Let me see her in person now," I said, not even trying to hide my anxiousness.

"Follow me," he said, then let us through the shop that was filled with nothing but exotics.

Just seeing all those cars made me wanna sell dope until I died. I spotted a Bentley GTC and fell in love at first sight. I ran my hand across it and really got to debating on buying that instead. It cost around two hundred thousand dollars. I knew from seeing it on the internet. Then we passed a two-tone Wraith that really got my blood flowing. I knew that ran for about four hundred fifty thousand dollars and I thought about clearing the safes out for that bitch.

"I'm coming back for that Wraith, Gino," I promised him and myself.

"I'll have it waiting for you."

"Gino, on my dead homies, I got that price tag sitting in my safe right now. I'll go clear that shit out." I let him know it was real with me. I wasn't lying, either. I had a lil' over a mill to my name stashed in my safes. I didn't wanna spend half my worth on a car, but my ego was fuckin' with me.

"Mr. Anderson, I believe you," he said, then put his hands in the air in surrender. "I wasn't being sarcastic at all. If I know one thing, it's that you're about your money and your word. When you're ready to buy it, you know I'm going to take care of you."

I let it go, cause before I could reply we stopped in front of the most beautiful car in the world to me. Some cars cost more, some were faster, but none were more beautiful. I rubbed my hand across the hood and I swear I could feel it trying to communicate with me. Energy shot throughout my entire body. I knew everything there was to know about that car, I loved it. I crouched down and kissed the door.

Tamia sucked her teeth. "Get a room." She sounded jealous.

I stood up and admired the new 2017 Maserati Gran Turismo. It was all white, cocaine white to be exact. The insides were damu red looking like a nigga blew his brains out on the seats. That's what we called suicide guts. The car was a beast. It looked like a 'great white' shark sitting on land. That pretty muthafucka was my dream car and I had just copped it.

"So, I take it you're in love and still wanna go through with the sale?" Gino asked, knowing damn well I was leaving with that car.

"Yeah, Tamia gone handle the paperwork as usual," I answered, then got in the driver's seat.

Tamia screwed her face up, then disappeared in the back with Gino. Bleed hopped in the passenger seat and leaned back getting real comfortable.

"I can get use to this, on me," he said sounding like he was getting ready to go to sleep.

"Your future is yo hands, my nigga. You wanna live like a king or die a mere mortal. Me, I'm about to run it up on these broke niggas." I was really feeling myself.

"How much this cost blood?"

"$132,000 for the whip, my nigga. The rest he put in his pocket, but that's the way it goes when you playing at this level. He gone make it look like it's Tamia car and she's paying monthly installments."

"I'm coming to get me one of these Bentleys in six months, and I'm not playing. Fuck those old schools and shit," he declared.

I burst out laughing at how serious he was and how fast he had changed up.

"I'm bout to have my man's out there in the North, bulletproof this muthafucka. Let's see 'em shoot this one up. And the bitches... they gone be like whoever behind that tent is a bad muthafucka." We started laughing together.

Tamia and Gino came back to the car about thirty minutes later. She looked frustrated, but he looked like it was Christmas and I felt like I was Big Meech.

"Everything is in order, Mr. Anderson. Now, would you like for me to give you all the details of the car? Kinda like a post sales pitch?"

"Twenty-inch chrome rims that come stock. It goes zero to sixty in a lil' less than four seconds, and it makes out at one hundred and eighty-eight miles per hour. I know my shit, now toss those keys." I laid it on real thick.

When we finally made it outside the sun was still shining real bright and it seemed like the Maserati grill had a mouth full of diamonds. No lie, it looked like the whole car was sparkling.

It was a perfect day that presented the perfect opportunity for me to do what I did best, show off. I parked the Maserati right in front of the Camaro and we had them positioned facing each other, right in the middle of the lot. I gave Tamia my phone and then it was on as soon as she pressed record. I looked directly at the camera and did what I do best.

Marcellus Allen

"Yeah, y'all niggas know who this is. This Big O-Dawg from the Mob Life on you bitch ass niggas. From now on, y'all call me Maserati O. Y'all see this twenty seventeen Gran Turismo lookin' like a shark on land, huh? Ho ass niggas, shot up the beamer, I didn't cry about it, I just went and dropped a buck fifty on a Rati, huh!" I yelled.

Then I started running my hands across the door real slow like I wasn't in no rush. Then, I bent down and kissed the rims for show.

"That's alright though cause I'm bout to bulletproof this bitch. Let's see y'all shoot this one up! I still got my sling on my arm and I already just copped this bitch just to make y'all crabs mad. Oh, and by the way, that lil' stunt y'all pulled with my bitch in the car, just cost y'all. The gloves are off now," I spat, then walked back to the front of the car standing next to Bleed.

"My shooter, Bleed, home and he already in that new Camaro. We gone see y'all real soon, maybe tonight," I probably shouldn't have said that last part.

When we pulled out the lot and got to the light, Bleed had the audacity to pull up next to me and crank his engine up. I rolled the window down and looked at him like he was crazy with a grin on my face, "You don't want those problems," I told him.

"We'll see when we touch the freeway, nigga," he said, then flipped me off before rolling his window back up.

I looked over at Tamia. "Put yo seat belt on, baby. It's about to get real."

She kicked her heels off instead. "I'm good, I trust you, daddy." She reclined back in her seat.

I loved the way the Maserati felt when I drove it. I couldn't feel the ground. It felt like we were floating on thin air. A nigga couldn't tell me nothing.

As soon as we got on the freeway we got right to it, no hesitation. The freeway was mostly empty since rush hour traffic hadn't kicked in yet. That was even better cause I got to

110

really perform on that nigga. Even with one arm in a sling, that nigga couldn't fuck with me or my Maserati. I don't know what he was thinking. His Camaro was holding his own for a while, but it's only so much he could do when going up against the beast I was in. Once I hit that one hundred mph mark, it was over for him. He was about twenty feet behind me and looked like he had just hit eighty mph.

"We bout to see what this bitch can really do, baby girl," I told Tamia, then turnt it up.

I hit one hundred twenty miles per hour on that nigga and he was officially out of the race, but once I hit 150 mph, it was just overkill. My heart was pounding out of my chest and my adrenaline was through the roof as I started to decrease the speed. Tamia was having the time of her life in that passenger's seat. She had the window all the way down so her long ass hair could fly all over the place with a huge smile on her face. She was yelling the whole time I was whippin' it, really enjoying herself.

"Where you tryna' go?" I asked once I had got back to a normal speed and Bleed was no longer in sight.

"Home," she answered.

"Aight," I responded, then put on Kevin Gates 'Ain't Too Hard.'

When we pulled into the parking garage to the condo, I turned the music off and faced her. "You done having an attitude? Cause I'm not about to go in here to argue with you."

"I've been having an attitude cause I need some dick, but that's about to be over now," she said, then started peeling her clothes off.

"Oh, you ain't forgot about the ritual?" I teased while taking my sling off. Every time I bought a new car we would get it in to break it in. That was our ritual.

I pulled my sweats down and leaned my seat back as she got on top of the dick. She eased her way down on it real slow while I spread her cheeks. She moaned out as I filled her up and that was all the motivation I needed. I positioned my hips and then leaned up off the seat, so I could really dig in her. She accepted the challenge and started throwing it down on me harder. She leaned in wrapping her arms around my neck and the head rest for more support and went to work on me. I decided to just give in, lay back and enjoy the ride.

"That's what I thought," she taunted.

"We'll see when I hit it from the back," I threatened.

She started going ham on me, riding like her life depended on it. The car was filled up with loud smacking sounds as our skin kept slamming into each other.

She leaned in closer to my neck and moaned out, "I'm bout to cum!" Then she started biting my neck.

I spread her cheeks again and started thrusting up, trying to hit her spot.

"Cum for daddy," I growled in her ear.

"Oh! Oh! I'm cumming!" she yelled.

I dug in deeper with each stroke until she got real still coating my meat with her juices. Then, she sprung back to life, jumping up and down on my dick for another five minutes until it was time for me to blast off.

"Aghh! I roared, as I shot the whole load inside of her. We laid there catching our breath for a few minutes then went inside to get round two jumping off.

Steady Mobbin'

Chapter 10
June 1st that night

We were back on our bullshit that night, locked and loaded and ready to kill somebody. Burnside had been doing his homework for a month, just for that occasion that we were on. It took forever for the nigga to get the info, but it couldn't of came at a better time. My heart was pumping evil through it for revenge. For that bullet that almost killed my bitch.

"You sure we can trust this bitch? I mean all of a sudden, she wanna give the info up. This might be a set up," I said to Burnside from the back seat. Bleed was back there next to me and Jersey Joe was riding shotgun.

"I think we good, blood. The nigga done fully cut her off and now she scorned. Plus, that five grand made her feel better," he replied.

"Well, break it down to me again so *I'll* feel better," I said.

"My lil' sister got a homegirl named Rebecca who used to mess with this fuck boy. They been off and on for a while, but he finally cut her off all the way for his baby mama. The nigga done made her get hella abortions, while he was playing house and that's what really did it. I've been tryna' get the info but she was holding out hoping that he takes her back, but no dice," he explained. It all made sense to me.

We turned down Fesseden Street and slowed down looking for the right house. It was a pretty decent neighborhood out there in North Portland, but we were about to turn it ugly.

"Word is bond! That's the niggas truck right there!" Joe pointed out excitedly.

Burnside just kept on driving like he didn't hear him. I looked over at Bleed who just shrugged his shoulders at me. He drove another block, then pulled over.

"That's his truck, but he always be in that beige Jaguar and it wasn't in the driveway," Burnside spoke up.

"How you know his bitch ain't got the Jag, son?" Joe questioned him.

"Blood, it's after eleven o'clock at night. Is you gone let yo baby mama be out?" Burnside explained his theory.

"Yeah, son, you right, so is we going in or are we waiting?" Joe wanted to know.

"We wait until he comes, then rush the nigga," I spoke.

Joe turned around. 'Naw, son, we should wait in the house for the nigga."

"Too loud if we kick the door down and wait, it'll fuck everything up," I tried to explain to him.

He shook his head and mumbled under his breath. "West Coast niggas under his breath."

I see what Bobbie been talking about now, I thought to myself. I didn't know what that nigga trip was, but I was only going to take so much of it. We pulled back up on the block and deaded the lights a few houses down from his.

"Yo, put that Kevin Gates on, blood," I told Burnside, after a few minutes of waiting.

"Hell naw, that's all you wanna listen to, Hood! I'm bout to put that Mozzy on, if anything. We can listen to Gates when we in your car, fuck that." Everybody started laughing at the truth.

"Fuck y'all niggas," I shot back.

He put the Mozzy on and we all just kicked back, soaking up the killer shit he was rapping about. That nigga did know how to put a nigga in killer mode, but the minute 'Sleep Walkin' went off, I was definitely ready to knock a nigga's head off behind this Mob shit!

About thirty minutes later, we watched the white Jaguar creep down the block. We all crouched down out of habit, even though we were behind tint.

Take a deep breath, You know what you're doing, I reminded myself.

As soon as the car door opened up, we were on his ass. He got out with his phone in his hand, sending a text message. *You just fucked up,* I thought to myself. We were damn near across the street and a few feet from him by the time he got the chance to look our direction. He froze up when he realized what time it

114

was. His eyes almost popped out of his head and he dropped his phone. His hand moved towards his waist out of habit, but he knew better than that.

"Go ahead, so I can knock yo head off yo shoulders," I threatened with my .40 aimed right at his face.

"Fuck!" was all he could say.

"If you make us kill you right here, then we gone go in there and kill ya whole family, yo choice!" I gave the ultimatum.

"Lead the way, crab," Burnside growled, then picked the phone up.

Dirty Dan led us in the house right after Joe stripped him of his pistol. My heart was beating fast as we walked through the door. We had finally caught one of their main niggas and I couldn't wait to kill his ass and find the rest of those pussies.

"Who else in here?" I asked his bitch ass.

"Just my baby mama and daughter. Man, what y'all niggas want, cuz?" he had the heart to ask.

Smack!

Bleed hit him on the head with the heat forcing him to crumble to the floor.

"First off, you ain't runnin' nothing just cause we in yo house. Second off, next time you smuz me I'ma knock yo noodles out, crab ass nigga," I checked him, then turned to Joe. "Go get the bitch, blood."

I crouched down next to Dirty Dan who was holding his bloody head. I got real close up on him, so he could read my eyes. I wanted him to see the demons inside of me.

"You, hoe ass niggas shot me. That's cool, it's part of war, but y'all grazed my wife in the head, now this shit is personal. Summin' tells me I should kill yo baby mom right now. What you think?" I spat.

Joe lead a half-naked sista down the stairs, who looked like she was ready to piss on herself and cry at the same time. She was pretty, but she chose the wrong side.

"What yo cracker ass doing with a Black bitch for a baby mom? I should kill her race trading ass on GP," Burnside spat, being dead serious. That nigga was the most racist nigga that I knew.

"See, son, this the shit I be talkin' about with you West Coast niggas. This type of shit would never fly in Jersey, word is bond. Got black bitches fuckin' with white devils and shit, son." Joe felt the need to West Coast bash.

"Man, shut the fuck up. Ain't nobody tryna' hear that New Jersey Drive bullshit. You niggas copy everything from us, go get ya own gangs, ya weak ass niggas!" Burnside shot at him.

"Yo', son, we make this shit look better and y'all stole rap from us! Fuck you talkin' bout?" Joe turned to him, forgetting all about the female.

"Yo' Tupac and Biggie! This ain't the time," I jumped in or they woulda' been arguing all night. That was their favorite thing to argue about.

"We gone finish this in the car." Burnside just had to have the last word.

"Tell me where Butta and Pressha live at or I'ma smoke ya bitch," I threatened.

"Fuck you, niggas, I ain't tellin' y'all shit! No snitchin' in my veins, cuz. You gone kill me anyways, so fuck y'all!" he yelled with his chest puffed out. *White boy got heart*, I thought to myself. Most niggas woulda' caved in at the thought of their baby mama getting killed. *Fuck it, the brave die young.*

"That's yo word? Watch this." Joe put his burner to the woman's head.

"Naw, don't kill her," I yelled out, before he could end her. He looked at me like I was going soft or something.

"The white nigga got heart, we can respect that," I said to Joe, then crouched back down facing Dan. "Give up the money and we'll spare yo bitch and the kid," I offered him.

"Give them the money, Daniel!" his bitch yelled out, crying at the mention of their child.

"Listen to yo' bitch or I'ma go get yo' son and blow his head off in front of you," I growled at him.

I saw the look of defiance mixed with defeat all over his face. He knew it was over, he was going to die that night. His eyes darted from left to right a few times, so I could tell he was debating something within himself. Go for it or give in, fight or flight. We all had to decide at some point in our lives.

"I'll give it to y'all, just please don't kill us. I know where it's at!" she blurted out after she seen him taking too long.

"Take me to it now!" Joe demanded, then followed her back up the stairs.

"Y'all really thought y'all was gone get away with that lil' stunt?" I said, then lifted that nigga's Gutta Squad chain off his neck. Them niggas had some fly ass chains, I couldn't deny them that. They looked like the old G-Unit spinning pieces but had GS in the middle, in all diamonds. I handed it over to Burnside, who put it on with a smile on his face.

"How I look?" he asked.

"Like a bitch ass nigga," I answered, then we broke out laughing.

"See a Gutta chain have Burnside take that shit," I taunted.

"Fuck y'all niggas cuz, y'all dead men walking," he spat, still wanting to be a brave-heart.

Joe came back, following behind the chick with a duffle bag over his shoulder. "You did good, sweetheart," I told her, then raised my gun right at her heart.

Boc! Boc! Boc!

She fell down slow, with a confused look on her face. She thought she was going to live to see another day.

"Bitch nigga!" Dirty Dan yelled, while trying to lunge at me.

Boom! Boom! Boom! Boom!

Bleed hit him all in the back dropping him on his stomach instantly. Burnside aimed at his head even though he wasn't moving.

Boom! Boom!

His head opened up, squirting blood everywhere.

Boca!

Joe shot the dead bitch for no reason in her chest. He looked at me like the shit was normal.

"Next body on me, dawg, no excuses," he had the nerve to mis quote Mozzy. The baby started crying and that's when we made our exit.

When we were away from the crime scene, I called Butta's on speakerphone. I couldn't deny myself the opportunity of taunting his fat ass.

"When yo scary ass gone leave the house and come meet me?" he said, as soon as he picked up.

That shit made my blood boil. "I actually just left ya man's Dirty Dan's house. It went pretty well," I spat.

"Cuz, stop calling my phone lyin' and I can't wait to catch you in that new Maserati."

"Pressha ho ass grazed my bitch in the head, so now the gloves are off. That's why I just killed Dan's baby mama. Y'all wanna keep playing this game? You might wanna get over there and get the baby, and the next time y'all do some shit like that, we gone start killin' the kids!" I hung up.

Just hearing that nigga voice had got me mad. I called to get under his skin, but he managed to do the same to me. What really had me hot was how arrogant he sounded about the shit. His bitch ass wasn't even no killer like that. Hell, he wasn't even the one that shot me. All he did was get money and feed the wolves. That nigga, Pressha, was the real killer and leader of their shit, but Butta controlled the money.

The funny thing was, the only reason Butta had the money was cause his grandparents died and left him hella money and a house. He took that money and started supplying the dope in the city. I wasn't trippin' cause I told myself that him and his niggas would be mourning, come the morning.

June 3rd

118

Steady Mobbin'

It had been a few days since the murders and those niggas hadn't done shit. I mean the usual shit happened, you know, threats on Facebook, dry snitchin' on Instagram, all that police shit. The news had been all over it, though, since it involved an innocent woman, but even that started dying down. Gang task was pulling niggas over left and right on some harassment type of shit. Just to act like they were doing something. Those pussies being real quiet did kinda make me nervous. I kept telling myself they were plotting something big.

I couldn't stay in the house forever. I had to get back to the money, plus the 'Rati' was finished getting bullet-proofed, and I needed to show off. My man, Mike, hit me up talking about he wanted a whole thang this time, so I had to go get the money. Bobbie had re-up'd with my brother while I was in Atlanta, so I had to move them pies I'd been sitting on since I got shot.

I pulled to the old Mr. Burger's parking lot on 42nd Killingsworth Street and parked while I waited for the nigga. We had never met there before since we always did it in his hood on a residential block and I wondered why the switch up. *Nigga better not be snitchin',* I thought, as I jumped out of the shark on land. It was a sunny Saturday and I'd be damned if I wasn't about to be seen.

Mike pulled in a few minutes later and hopped out lookin' all scared and shit. I knew we were facing fed time, but damn. I leaned against the hood, while I waited for him to reach me.

"Damn, blood, you don't think you a lil' hot standing out like that?" he asked while he was looking around, all nervous and shit.

"Feds ain't expecting a nigga to move like this. That's why I do it, we good. Plus, I'ma be fly as hell if the feds watchin'," I said mimicking the song.

"Let's do this," he said as he tried to hand me the bag.

"Throw it in the trunk and grab yo shit outta there," I told him, then I popped the trunk while watching him real closely.

He did it, then, with a weird look on his face. he said, "Aight, my nigga, I'll holla at you next time."

119

"Hop in and let me holla at you real quick, my nigga." I watched him reluctantly get in. "The whole twenty-eight thousand in there, right?" I asked.

"Come on, O, you know I wouldn't play with you like that."

"I know, but this vibe I'm getting from you is making me real nervous," I said, then put the pistol on my lap with my hand on the trigger. "You care to calm my nerves, or you gone play dumb?" I called him out.

He looked from the gun to my eyes and could obviously see I was dead serious.

"The homies are trippin' with you and talkin' about niggas can't do business with you no more," he confessed.

"And why is that?" I asked, hella confused as to what he meant.

"Because of Keisha."

"Who the fuck is Keisha?" I frowned.

"You really don't know?" He sounded confused, then put his face in his hands and started shaking his head. "Keisha was Dirty Dan's baby mama who just happen to be Big Floyd's niece," he finally spat it out, then looked in my eyes for any signs of guilt.

That shit hit me like a ton of bricks right in the gut. The last thing I felt like doing was going to war with the Murda Squad Piru's and that's what Mike was basically telling me was inevitable. It wasn't that those niggas was just some niggas not to be fucked with. It was that they were my niggas. I didn't want beef with no other Bloods, but that was looking real likely at that moment. Big Floyd was basically their leader, so whatever he felt like doing, they were all going to follow him.

"So, what's the move. Y'all niggas wanna talk or what, or is it already a green light?" I asked, ready to kill that nigga right then and there.

"All I know is that we're supposed to have the candlelight today, then the funeral in a few days, then come holla at y'all," he said.

120

Steady Mobbin'

"When y'all ready to talk after the funeral, we'll be ready. Hopefully, we can get all this shit squashed," I told him.

"Whatever happens, I want you to know that I ain't in it. You always done put money in my pocket when those niggas wouldn't. If shit pop off, I'ma be on the side lines," he said, then shook me up, before he jumped out and rushed back to his whip.

I pulled off with a lot on my mind and was deciding how to deal with it all. No matter what idea I came up with, it ended with war at the end of the day. I got mad at Burnside for not doing his homework all the way, but figured that wasn't gone change nothing. We were just gone have to deal with it like we did everything else. Steady Mob on it.

I called Bobbie, yelling in the phone.

"Blood, we gotta meet up right now and talk cause you ain't never gone believe this shit!"

A few hours later, Bobbie was riding shotgun in the 'Rati' and we had five cars tailing us to our destination. We were all posted up at the Mob quarters, breaking down the situation when Burnside suggested that we just push up on those niggas right now and from there it was all downhill.

We called our lil' niggas, strapped up and got on with the business. Personally, I thought we should have waited until emotions weren't running so high, but the wolves were hungry, so that's what it was.

Soon as we got a couple blocks from Peninsula Park, that's when the blocks became crowded with parked cars. I knew at that moment, there was going to be way too many people out there. We were already there though, and it was on.

"You sure this is just hers? Cause if their being done together, then that means those crabs are gone be out here too and this is way too many people for a shootout," I told Bobbie while driving past the entrance.

"Naw, it's just hers. Her family been all on Facebook blaming Dan for her being dead and his family on there arguing back at them. They definitely ain't rockin' right now," he explained to me.

I parked across the street at the corner store and hopped out while all my niggas did the same thing. We were about twenty deep and quickly filled up the parking lot. Everybody that was standing at the entrance to the park immediately started shooting daggers in our direction.

I watched a few of them head inside the park, no doubt going to get those niggas. We stood around for a few minutes just leaning on our cars looking at the the watchers.

"Fuck it, let's just go over there," Gotti said and he was usually the calm one.

"If they ain't coming to us than we goin' to them. You ready, O?" Burnside instigated.

"Let's go then," I said, after thinking about it for a second.

We crossed the street, looking like we were about to start shooting, with mugs on our faces and hands by our hips. If anything looked funny, we would have got to bustin' and that's why I didn't wanna actually go inside the park. It was a few young niggas standing behind a table that had candles and pictures of her, all throughout her life. Them niggas looked like they had something on their minds.

"What's good with y'all, fam?" I asked the group.

They just stared through us with hate for a few seconds, then one finally spoke up. "Y'all can't come in here, blood."

"Lil' nigga, you must not know who you talkin' to. This my city and I go where the fuck I want to. Now, which one of y'all gone stop me?" I challenged, as I took a few steps closer.

"Here they come," Gotti said, snapping me out of the zone that I was getting into.

"About time," I replied, then took my attention away from those punks and onto the real threat.

Big Floyd and a group of his people came walking up with screwed up faces like they were hard or summin'. Their whole demeanor screamed hostility, but that was fine with us, we had come prepared for that.

Steady Mobbin'

"So, you niggas wanna be disrespectful, blood?" His voice boomed when he got within a couple feet of us.

"Blood, you better lower yo fuckin' voice when you talkin' to a killer. I ain't one of yo' weak ass lil' homies, nigga," I spat fire from my mouth. I was mad as hell that this nigga tried to front on me.

"Lower my voice? You niggas come to my relative's candlelight after y'all kill her and you tell me to lower my voice? You lil' niggas are brave!"

"How you just gone say we killed yo people without talkin' to me first?" I sounded offended.

"Because Butta told me all about your lil' call and showed me the call log. You called four minutes after neighbors reported the shots. Y'all did it, blood," he stated the facts with conviction.

"So, since you're so convinced, what you want to do about it?" I got straight to the point, tired of playing games with the nigga.

He shrugged his shoulders. "Life for a life. Bring me the nigga that pulled the trigger and we avoid going to war," he said matter of factly.

"You make it sound like going to war is in y'all nigga's favor. My bitch got shot in the head, so from now on ain't nobody safe. You should of stopped fuckin' with a weak ass crab," I spat, full of venom.

"So, what you sayin', nigga?" he tensed up.

"You know what the fuck we sayin', son!" Joe yelled out, then knocked all the candles and pictures off the table. "Fuck that dead bitch and fuck Piru. Now what's poppin'?" he screamed in their faces to everybody's surprise.

Those niggas stood still, in total shock for a second, then tried to rush us like we were all about to fight. We pulled those pistols out, and aimed them at their faces, so fast, they didn't know what to do. I had mine aimed straight at Big Floyd's forehead.

"The cops are on the way! You niggas going to jail!" A lady yelled out from the park.

Marcellus Allen

I looked around and noticed dozens of people staring at us from inside the park. *Not right now,* I told myself.

"Next time you see me, you better kill me," I said then kicked one of the fallen pictures at those niggas' feet.

"Next time you pull a gun, use it, lil' niggas," he shot back, wanting to sound tough.

"I did last time."

I left him with something to think about. Something that was gone hit him in the gut as he laid in the bed that night. We were some disrespectful niggas.

Steady Mobbin'

Chapter 11
June 6th

"You can huff and puff all you want, Olay, but yo ass ain't going nowhere," I told her, while pacing the room frustrated.

A lot of shit had gone down in the following days after that candle light situation. Those Gutta Squad niggas stopped acting like hos and was tryna' bring it to us. I could respect that. Those Murda Piru niggas were tryna' slide on the low too, as expected. It was heavy around that time out there in the streets. I'm talking five or six shootouts a day, every day. We lost two of our lil' niggas in that short period.

Niggas were all over the internet talking about killing my baby mama for that Keisha bitch. All them pussies were doing was making it harder on themselves and their loved ones. I wasn't concerned with those internet thugs or their dry threats, but Olay was. She was back on her trip that day talkin' about she was moving to California.

"Yes, I am, Marshawn! I don't feel safe here anymore and I'm tired of this shit. Random people on Facebook talking about killing my family. How you think I'm supposed to feel? We're not safe here, Marshawn," she pleaded her case.

"We are safe, this my city," I arrogantly stated.

"You have a fuckin' bulletproof vest on inside the house. How are we safe? We live in a gated community and you're in here ready for war, in our house!"

I looked down at my vest, then at the gun on my waist. She did have a point about that. I was definitely living on the edge and stayed ready at all times, but fuck that, I wasn't tryna' let her leave.

"We're safe, Olay, and I'll always protect you," I told her calmly.

"Like we were safe the day this happened?" She parted her hair to show me the scar that the bullet had left. "I feel *real* protected!" she screamed at me.

Boom!

Marcellus Allen

I punched a hole in the wall making her jump back a few feet. Just the thought of that night made me start seeing red. I was ready to go kill somebody at that moment. I was even more mad that she had the heart to throw that shit in my face like that. Now my pride was hurt more than anything.

"I'ma go to the basement before I forget how much I love you, but since you wanna disrespect me, go ahead and leave, but don't touch my son," I said.

I shot downstairs before I messed around and put my hands on her. I was that mad. All the shit I'd done for her in my life and she really questioned my heart like that. I covered her up when those shots were ringing out and when we were getting ready to crash. I did that shit out of instinct, in the heat of the moment. I was hurt by what she said and how she said it, but I think what hurt the most was that it had some truth to it.

I was playing a game of pool by myself when she made her way down there about an hour later. I didn't even acknowledge her. We didn't have nothing to talk about. I just kept on playing like she wasn't even there. *Fuck this bitch,* I said to myself.

"So, you're not going to talk to me?" she asked with attitude.

I kept on playing like I didn't hear her say a word. She walked over and started slapping the balls everywhere.

"I'm scared, Marshawn!" she screamed at me, then started punching my vest with tears streaking down her face.

I wrapped her in my arms real tight and pressed her head against my chest letting her cry for a few minutes. I rubbed her back and just let her get it all out. It pained my heart to hear the woman of my life crying in my chest out of fear. To hear the mother of my son tell me that she's scared to live in her own city. *I'ma kill those niggas,* I said to myself. At the moment, I felt the devil consuming me. This war was no longer business, it was personal.

"I'm sorry for saying that to you. I didn't mean it like that," she apologized still sobbing.

"It's okay, wifey, don't worry about it. I think it's best if you do go to Cali for a few weeks and prepare for that tournament, but not to live. Just stay about a month to focus and spend my money."

She started laughing, then punched me.

"Leave Mar-Mar at my mom's house. She's been wanting to spend time with him anyways. When you get back, we'll talk again, aight?" I said, then kissed her.

"Okay, daddy, that sounds good," she replied.

"Finish packing, I got some stuff I need to handle, baby," I told her, then sat on the couch with a heart full of anger.

A few hours later we were riding around two cars deep, but we weren't on no killer shit that night. We were just going to the strip club to unwind, cause it had been a long week, and I mean a long one. It seemed like it had been forever since we just went out to have fun and that's why we decided to go do it. Plus, I needed to see some ass and titties to keep my mind off that shit with Olay from earlier that day.

"I'm telling you, my nigga, that shit really broke my heart. Hearing wifey cry like that. I can't wait to kill those niggas, blood," I vented to Bobbie, who was sitting in the passenger's seat.

"I can't imagine," was all he said. He wasn't being cold, he was dead serious. He'd never had a main chick that he loved, he didn't believe in that. He just tricked off a lil' and left it at that.

"Don't trip, lil' bro, my baby mama been on the same shit. It just comes with the territory. She'll be aight," Gotti said from the back seat.

I nodded my head hoping he was right, cause I needed Olay with me every day. I couldn't imagine her living in another state. That wasn't gone happen.

We got to the strip club and it was poppin' so heavy in the parking lot that we jumped out the 'Rati' before I could find a parking spot. Burnside, Jersey Joe and Trell hopped out the Benz right behind us. That's how it usually was at Majic Monroes, live and off the chain. It was bad bitches standing everywhere and we were on them.

"Burnside, when you gone come fuck with me?" some light skinned female blurted out.

We all looked in her direction, so we could focus on her friends to see if they were worth our time. They all looked good to me, so I was with it.

"See what's good wit' 'em," I told Burnside.

"Yo, who that?" he yelled back, as we made our way towards the group.

She smacked her lips. "Don't play with me, boy. It's Sabrina."

"Oh Brina? What's poppin' wit y'all?" he asked when we got right on them.

Sabrina was standing with a group of about eight bitches that all looked reputable and were giving us their undivided attention. I had seen a few of them around the way and on Facebook but had never talked to any of them.

"Nothing, tryna' get in this club. What's up with y'all," she shot back.

"Look, we tryna' do the same thang as y'all. So why don't y'all come link up with us in VIP and we can all get to know each other," I jumped in, shooting my shots.

"Umm, that sounds good to me," her thick ass dark skinned friend spoke up.

"Say that then. What's your name though?" I asked.

"Remy, what's yours?" she answered stepping closer in my face.

"They call me O-Dawg," I said real slow, just so I could watch her facial expression change from curiosity to lust. It never failed.

"Oh, I know who you are," she said with her mouth wide open. She looked me up and down, real slow. "You be rapping and stuff, right?" she asked, fronting like a muthafucka.

"Yo, O! You gone leave yo car right here runnin' or what?" the security yelled over to me.

"Walk with me real quick," I told her, then headed to my car.

128

Steady Mobbin'

I walked up to the security guard and dapped him up cause he could of got on some hater shit in a few different ways, but they knrw me there, so they treated me like royalty.

"My bad, big man, for just leaving it right there blocking traffic and shit" I slid him a twenty-dollar bill.

"Not a problem, just didn't want you to leave it and somebody try to steal it," he said, causing us both to laugh at the odds of that happening.

"Is this a Maserati?" Remy asked, not able to hide her excitement.

"That's exactly what it is, baby girl," I replied with arrogance.

"Oh my God! I've never been inside one of those before," she said drooling over the car.

Me and the security looked at each other thinking the same thing, she was gone be down for whatever after the club.

"Well, now you have. Go park it for me!" I said feeling myself way too much.

"Are you serious?" she yelled, but opened the door after I nodded at her. "Why is this door so heavy. It's hard to pull it," she said, while she struggled with it then finally got inside.

"Cause it's bulletproof, for a bulletproof type of nigga," I answered being my usual cocky self as we watched her struggle a lil' bit to close the door.

"What if she crash yo shit?" he asked with a smirk on his face.

"Then that twenty I gave you ain't gone compare to the ten thousand I'ma pay you to say I was never here. Cause I'ma kill that bitch." I was dead serious.

"Then I hope she crashes it," he joked.

Baby girl parked it just fine and hopped out with the biggest smile on her face while she walked over. I couldn't blame her cause I felt the same way when I first parked it.

We walked inside the club and it was definitely just as poppin' in there as it was outside, if not more. It felt like all eyes were on us as we made our way to the VIP balcony, but that was

129

the usual anyways. A few of the niggas I made eye contact with looked like they were surprised to see me. I gripped that .40 just to make sure it was in place. I wasn't worried about nothing.

"What would you like for me to get y'all?" a half-naked bottle girl asked me after escorting us to VIP.

"Bring me a bottle of that Moet Rose' and whatever they want. Just throw it on the tab," I told her, then gave my attention to Remy. "What's on your mind?" I asked.

"I was just thinking how cool you are. Every time I hear yo' name, it's got to do with a shooting or somebody dyin' or some wild shit, but all y'all just seem like regular niggas," she said.

I looked at her like she was crazy. "Never use the 'R' word around me again. I ain't nothing like them other niggas. I'm on a whole 'nother level, but as far as the shootings and shit, I don't know anything about that, baby girl." I smirked at her.

She rolled her eyes. "I didn't mean regular like that, I just meant y'all are real laid back and fun to kick it with," she explained herself.

A half hour later, all the bottles were half gone, and we were turnt up to the max throwing money everywhere. It seemed like all the baddest strippers had made their way to our section to get a bag full of that money we were throwing. Niggas couldn't tell us nothing, we were those niggas. Bobbie had came through too, with Falon on his arms and a few of our lil' niggas with him. Jersey Joe had a weird look on his face when they came in, too. I wondered if it was because Falon cut him off and he was salty about it. Every now and then I would catch him giving Falon the side eye.

Tossing him to the back of my mind for the moment, I stood up on the couch with a bottle of Rose' and screamed. "Now when I say Mob, y'all say life!"

"Mob!" I yelled.

"Life!" they shouted back.

"Mob!" I yelled again.

"Life!" everybody yelled. The strippers, the homies, the bitches with us and even a few niggas and broads that were in the next section yelled out with us. Everybody wanted to be a part of the winning team. There was no mistake about it, the Mob ran Portland.

Burnside's crazy ass stood on top of the table with his arms spread out and a bottle in each hand. "From now on I'm from Gutta Squad as y'all can see from my chain!" he yelled, passing a bottle to the nearest stripper, so he could hold the Gutta Squad chain that was hanging from his neck in the air. "I'm the new capo of Gutta Squad and fuck y'all Mob niggas!" he yelled, then took a drink.

Everybody started throwing all types of shit at the nigga until he jumped down in defeat. We got back to throwing money and having the time of our lives. Remy was all over me, but I kept trying to brush her to the side cause I didn't feel like hearing Falon's mouth or have her tryna' blackmail me.

"I'm ready to leave whenever you are," Remy whispered in my ear and grabbed my dick.

"Aight, hold up!" I told her, then motioned for Bobbie to meet me in the corner.

"What's brackin', nigga?" he asked.

"Nigga, we tryna' take these bitches to the telly, but you got Falon's nosey ass in here. Take her with you to the car or summin'. I don't know why you brought her in the first place."

"I got you, blood," he replied, with a dumb ass smile on his face.

As I was watching Falon to make sure she didn't push up on Remy, I saw her texting in her phone real fast and suspicious looking. Then I looked over at Joe who was doing the same thing. *These dumb muthafuckaz,* I thought to myself.

"So, what's up with you and her anyways cause it sho' seem like y'all rockin'?" I asked to get a temperature check.

"It ain't shit to me, blood. Just fuckin' and spending money. I ain't putting no car seats in the back of my Benz." I knew he was dead serious.

If Bobbie didn't care, and I knew he didn't, then why the hell were they sneaking around, I thought to myself. I decided

131

to let it go for the time being but promised myself I was gone look more into it.

"Aight, well snatch Falon up and blow this joint so we can leave too. We gone be right behind you," I told him.

"Aight, blood, I'ma shake Falon, then slide to where y'all niggas is at," he said then we dapped up and he went to grab Falon.

I went back over and sat down next to Remy and Burnside who was whispering in her friend's ear. I was ready to slide to the hotel and get some of my pinned-up frustration sucked from me.

"What's good? Y'all tryna' blow this joint and hit the telly?" I asked interrupting their conversation.

"Let's be out, you wit it, baby?" Burnside asked his lil' work.

She nodded her head, as we all stood up to make our exit. Once the Mob left the building, the club was good as dead.

We hopped in our whips and headed to the 7/11 store, so we could grab a couple boxes of Swishers and some condoms, so we could get it in once we got there. The females were in their own cars following right behind us probably doing the same thing we were doing, talking about how it was about to go down.

"I'm telling y'all, blood, I'm bout to really get it in. That bitch was on me all night," Bleed declared from the backseat.

"I'm probably just gone get sucked up real quick, then head to the spot," Gotti said.

I just drove and listened to those niggas go back and forth for about ten minutes, until we pulled into the lot. Everybody hopped out the cars including the broads and either we went into the store or was posted up on the cars. Me, Trell, and Burnside went in the store together feeling ourselves and anxious to hurry up and get to the telly. Our plan was to get the Presidential Suite at the Red Lion Hotel and just get it poppin' everywhere in that bitch.

Steady Mobbin'

"Did you see how a few bitch niggas were looking all weird when I was showing the chain off?" Burnside asked, as we paid for our shit.

"Yeah, but they ain't wanna do nothing about it. They probably just groupie niggas, fuck em!" was Trell's reply.

"Nigga, that shit was hot, but it is what it is," I spoke up as we made our way to the door.

Soon as we walked outside, I heard a car come to a screeching stop and a voice yell out, "Gutta Squad!" and before we could even turn our heads, it was on.

Boc! Boc! Boc! Boc! Boc! Boc! Boc! Boc! Bap! Bap! Bap!

Trell got hit up and flew back into me. The force knocking us both to the ground with my arms wrapped around him.

Bap! Bap! Bap! Boc! Boc! Boc! Boc!

When I hit the ground, that's when I could actually see what was happening. Pull-Out and Ron were standing in front of a car that was in the middle of the street to the right side of us, gassin' us! Trell had me pinned to the ground, stuck. *Fuck that*, I told myself after I realized I had no time to get him off me. I yanked out and got to bussin' back, reaching around him.

Boom! Boom! Boom! Boom! Boom! Boom!

My aim wasn't the best, but them niggas knew I wasn't playing no games! All that kept going through my head was I ain't going out like this.

Blocka! Blocka! Blocka! Blocka! Bap! Bap! Boc! Boc! Boc! Bap! Bap! Bap! Blocka! Blocka!

I finally ended up rolling that nigga off of me and stood tall, like a real nigga. Jersey Joe was the only one returning fire and I joined the show. Before I could blink, everything was over, and I was shooting at the back of those niggas cars as they sped off.

Everybody stood up and rushed over to Trell who was dead to the world with his eyes still open. He had taken at least three to the chest and one to the neck.

We all lowered our heads and wiped at are teary eyes. Damn, my nigga was gone. They had struck back! I looked down at my clothes and they were soaked in blood from top to bottom.

"Agh shit!" I growled out, after I ran my hand over my chest and stomach.

"What's wrong, nigga?" Burnside started to panic.

I lifted my vest up and showed them the black and blue mark that was swelling on my stomach. These niggas had hit me, but the vest stopped the bullet. That's what made me fly to the ground like that. *I'ma kill those niggas,* I said to myself. We started hearing sirens everywhere snapping us back into reality reminding us that it was time to leave. I looked at my nigga one last time, really not wanting to leave him like that, but I had no choice.

"C'mon, nigga!" Gotti yelled, then started grabbing me by the arm.

"I'ma get those niggas for you," I whispered to Trell, then took off to the car.

The Next Day

Wasn't nothing to talk about, we were on our bullshit and that was that. Trell getting killed that night really fucked us up, especially me. He was a solid lil' nigga. So, we were about to turn the city up behind him. Not only did he put that work in for me about that snitch nigga, but he took a couple of bullets for me. I knew those niggas were gunnin' for me and he just happened to be positioned wrong. I didn't get no sleep that night. I kept seeing him lying dead on top of me. That was my first time holding a dead man. Them bitch ass niggas were probably celebrating all that night, but I promised to have them sick the next day.

So that's why we were three cars deep about to do the unthinkable. We had come up with a thousand different ways to hit those niggas back, but none of them sent a good enough message for me. I told everybody to keep thinking and that's when Jersey Joe said, "Let's shoot the funeral up."

Soon as the words left his mouth, they went straight to my heart and that was it.

We didn't really do the whole disrespectinga funeral thing, it's frowned upon. Shit, it hadn't happened since the nineties at that point, but we were in our feelings and the funeral was only hours away, so we said fuck it, why not? We knew they weren't going to be expecting it and that's exactly what I wanted. What really sealed the deal was when they bitch asses got on Facebook talkin' bout 'now Dan can rest in peace' and 'it's Dan's day.'

Okay, let's make it Dan's Day, I said to myself as I cocked the Mac 11 back.

"We gone fuck the Town up with this one, blood." I looked over to Bleed, who was sitting in the backseat with me.

"On me!"

"Yo, Bobbie, don't forget to slide this muthafucka back around either. I ain't playin' no games," I spat.

"I'm on it, blood, we almost there," Bobbie replied, then started slowing down.

I looked out the window and we were right on time. It was a bunch of people standing around looking all sad and shit. *I'ma make y'all really sad in a minute,*

It was hella packed out there but all I could see were women and lil' kids. I wanted them niggas! We kept on driving slow searching the crowd for our enemies. I knew them pussies were out there somewhere.

"Yo, there them niggas go!" Bobbie got all excited and started pointing up ahead.

I looked closely and saw a group of niggas standing by an Escalade looking like they were ready to ride right now. We were damn sho' bout to find out if they were really ready or not.

"That's Pull-Out, Ron, Half Dead and a bunch of other niggas I don't know," I responded.

"I want Butta and Pressha!" Bobbie replied, then started looking around for them.

"Me too, but I saw Pull-Out and Ron doing the shooting last night, so we on 'em," I declared then cocked the Mac 11 back.

Clack! Clack!

Soon as Bobbie got close enough, my heart got to beating faster. I put my new Jason mask on and it was beast mode after that.

I jumped out before he could come to a complete stop. *This for my dawg!*

"Mob up or lay down!" I yelled out the creed, then did what I did best.

Blatt! Blatt! Blatt!

Them niggas took off as soon as the flame got to jumping out the barrel. I guess they weren't as mad as they portrayed to be.

Boc! Boc! Boc! Boom! Boom! Doom! Doom! Doom! Bloc! Bloc! Bloc! Bloc! Blocka! Blocka!

Bleed and Bobbie jumped out letting their guns do the talking for them and less than a second later, I heard all the homies behind us start shooting too. It was bullets and bodies flying everywhere.

Blatt! Blatt! Boc! Boc! Boc! Boc! Blatt! Blatt!

The lil' nigga, Pull-Out, turned around after running for safety, then actually had the heart to shoot back at us!

Booyow! Booyow! Booyow!

His lil' ass got to buckin' a hand cannon at us tryna' knock summin' down. I lined him up perfect, then let loose on 'em.

Blatt! Blatt! Blatt! Booyow! Booyow! Blaatt! Blaatt!

He dropped to one knee from the bullets that tore his stomach and leg up, but just as fast as he hit the ground, he spun around shooting and running away.

Booyow! Booyow! Blatt! Blatt! Click! Click!

I went empty as his bitch ass escaped behind a car.

Boc! Boc! Boc! Boc! Boc! Boom! Boom! Boom! Boom! Blocka! Blocka! Blocka!

Steady Mobbin'

My niggas were still shooting at anything with two legs while everybody else was still running. I jumped back in the whip followed by my two niggas and we mashed out.

"Yo, hand me that 'K' and bend the block again!" I told Bobbie while popping another clip in the Mac 11. He handed it to me and I felt a rush of evil shoot through me.

"Who we lookin' for?" Bobbie asked after bending the block.

I looked around and only seen a bunch of innocent people getting up off the ground. Those pussies were gone, but that's not the only reason why I had him come back.

"Pull up next to the hearse," I demanded.

I knew since the funeral was over, that bitch nigga's body was laying in there. I was hell bent on showing those niggas what it felt like to be disrespected. *Y'all wanted to play games, let's play.* I hopped out aiming the AK right at the hearse.

Yoppa! Yoppa! Yoppa! Yoppa! Yoppa! Yoppa!

I swiss cheesed his punk ass again. Now he needed another funeral. Fuck that nigga and Gutta Squad.

"Be out! Be out!" I jumped in the car, yelling. We left out leaving tire marks and a cold story to tell.

Marcellus Allen

Chapter 12
June 8th

"Hello?" I answered my phone, half sleep and irritated from getting awakened out of a deep sleep.

"Turn on the news, blood!" Burnside yelled in my ear.

I hung up on that nigga then found the remote to turn the Fox 12 news on. The first thing I saw was the church and a whole bunch of yellow tape everywhere. There were crowds of people standing around looking distraught and some even had the audacity to try and look hard. *Niggas be killing me,* I thought to myself.

I turned the volume up and listened to the sexy ass reporter speak on some shit that she knew nothing about. Once I saw the bitch ass gang task Sergeant start talking in the mic, I turned the volume all the way up and sat up in the bed.

"We're going to catch these heartless criminals and throw them all in prison. They're punks who have no regard for human life, and cowards who shoot up funerals where innocent people are grieving," the Sergeant said. I cut him off, jumping out my bed.

"Bitch ass nigga! Coward? Aight, nigga, I'm on you now!" I yelled and pointed at the tv like he could hear or see me.

"We're doubling down on this one. I've instructed all my officers to do whatever is necessary to catch these cowards. Justice will be served, and arrests will be made," he promised.

I hit mute on his bitch ass then got real close, so we could be eye to eye.

"Nigga, fuck Gang Task! Y'all gone have to call in the National Guard for me, you hear? My lil' homie dead and y'all talkin' about we cowards? We gone see who the coward is, pussy. Tell the people the truth, nigga, y'all know who did it. The Mob did it! It ain't about what you know, it's what you can prove. Arrests? Who the fuck you gone arrest? Yeah, a'ight, just make sure y'all dress warm, pussy. I'm God out here, nigga!"

I yelled at his mark ass then turned the tv off. I sat back on the bed and started rolling some weed up. I needed to get high. I hated when muthafuckas threaten me. I didn't care who it was, bitch ass nigga, I thought to myself then took a long pull on the blunt.

"Here you go, Papi," Tamia said. She came in with my breakfast, just as I was finishing the blunt.

"Thank you, baby," I replied, then tapped her on the ass. She was only wearing a bra and panties, so I couldn't help it.

"I just seen on the news. They were talking about that funeral getting shot up. I hope that wasn't y'all. They sound real serious about putting them in jail. Summin' about one person dying and like seven being shot," she said, then looked at me with a questioning look. I looked at her once, then kept on eating my food like she ain't said nothing. "And who the hell you in here flashing on? I could hear you way in the kitchen."

"Nothing, baby, somebody said something that I ain't like. Thank you for the food, I appreciate it," I replied, trying to dismiss her.

My phone started ringing before she could find something else to question me about. I answered, already knowing who the caller was. "What's mobbin'? I'll be there in an hour," I said, then hung up. Tamia was still standing there. "Get dressed, we gotta go to my brother's house," I told her then finished eating my food.

Thirty minutes later, we arrived at my brother's spot. "I see you got ya vest on, huh? Y'all niggas out here heating the streets up, I see," Jaxx felt like being sarcastic, as I walked into his house. He threw a few punches at me and smirked.

"Yeah, it's real out here. Pop-A-Nigga Portland," I shot back as I sat on the couch.

My brother lit a blunt up, then just stared at me. I was used to his antics though, he'd been doing it since I was a kid. I already knew what was next and it was inevitable.

Steady Mobbin'

"See, I know what the problem is," he coughed, then passed the blunt. "Y'all out here listening to too much of that damn Mozzy. Now y'all wanna shoot up funerals and shit. Do this look like Flint, Michigan to you? Chiraq? You dumb ass niggas are going to jail, you know that right?"

I passed the weed back to him, so he would shut the fuck up. I knew exactly how to handle him.

"I want thirty from now on," I said, then leaned back with cockiness.

He stared at me for a few seconds then hit the blunt. "You want thirty thangs from now on?"

"That's what I said."

"So that's it, just give you thirty bricks. No talkin' about it, no explanation, just hand you the keys?" he replied sarcastically.

"I'm not asking you to give me anything, nigga. First off, I pay my way. I don't see no point in keep coppin' ten thangs when I got the money to get more, plus my nigga's appetites are getting bigger. I'm bout to run it up on these niggas, blood. I'm putting house on it. Give me a couple more weeks and I'ma be at fifty," I predicted.

"So, you really feeing yaself, huh? Shootings at the funeral, killing bitches, now you ready to up the order, huh? Aight, Scarface, I got you. Same rules, same prices."

I knew he was testing me. He knew damn well that the prices had to drop since I was coppin' more. "Cut the crap, bro. Lower the price and go get my shit. I got shit to do today." I stood up, letting him know I was done talking to his ass.

After my brother shot me my work, I took it straight to the Ville where I had my niggas waiting on me. Ever since those pussies tried to kill me at Tamia's old spot, I hadn't really slid through there. I would drive in and be gone within minutes. I didn't trust it no more, but fuck all that, I was back on my bullshit and I felt like letting niggas know what it felt like to see me jump out of a Maserati.

Plus, ever since that day, I had my niggas pushing the line on any nigga that lived in there that wasn't with us. Fuck all that neutral shit, Mob up or get shot down.

"So, this is what it is. We turnin' it up on these broke niggas," I told my homies after dumping the work on the table.

Burnside grabbed one off the table. "Good, cause I got a few niggas out in Seattle who been hittin' me up for some more thangs. I know just what to do with this." He rubbed his palms together.

Everybody started snatchin' the work up with smiles on their faces like they already had plans for them. The only one who didn't jump at the opportunity, was Bobbie. He sat there with a look of disgust written all over his face. He looked at each person then focused back on me.

"What's Mobbin'? You ain't tryna' get this money or summin'?" I asked, after looking from him to the dope left on the table then back up to him.

"I don't give a fuck about that money, nigga," he spat, then slapped a brick out of Burnside's hand.

"Lil' bro ain't even buried yet and y'all niggas in here with smirks on ya faces talkin' bout getting money. We ain't even killed one of those niggas that really matter to 'em, but y'all wanna celebrate and shit? I wonder how y'all gone act if I get killed," he said, making us sound like we didn't give a fuck about the homie.

I knew not to take that shit serious. That's just how he was. He stayed in full time gang bang mode. Plus, Trell was his favorite lil' nigga, so he was taking it extra hard.

"Nigga, you betta pick my dope up before I beat yo' ass," Burnside said, half-jokingly.

"I ain't picking up shit, nigga, make me," Bobbie spat then snatched his gun out the holster and dropped it on his lap.

We all looked at each other, then at Bobbie, then burst out laughing at how serious he was. We were high as a muthafucka and tryna' enjoy life and there that nigga was pulling out guns and shit for no reason.

142

Steady Mobbin'

"Yo' this nigga bout to shoot the house up," Gotti yelled out, then fell on the ground laughing, holding his stomach.

"This nigga trippin', blood," Burnside said, then picked the bird up, still laughing.

I looked at Bobbie and could see that he really felt some type of way about everything. Wasn't nothing gone make him feel better, except gun play.

"Don't trip, blood. Me, you and Bleed gone go get on summin' later on. Plus, them Piru niggas be talkin' reckless on the net. We can go slide on those niggas too," I told him to make him calm down a lil' bit.

"Yeah, blood, we ain't done rydin' for the homie, don't trip. You need to go home and fuck Falon thick ass. That's what I would do if I had that bitch. I would never leave the house, on me!" Bleed added his opinion, making everybody start laughing.

Joe was the only nigga that didn't laugh. *This nigga bet not still feel no type of way about this bitch,* I said to myself.

"Yo, I'm about to slide out. I'ma get with y'all later on tonight," I told my niggas, then shook each one up before I left.

An hour later, I pulled up to my mama's house to check on her and my son. She stayed in the suburbs way out in Troutdale which was more than good with me, but damn, I hated driving way out there. I walked in the house and saw my mother laying on the couch watching TV. She smiled and sat up when she saw me walk in. I gave her a kiss then sat down next to her.

"Hey, baby." She smiled wider.

"What's going on, Mama? Where my bad son at?" I asked, looking around for him.

"Pssh, I finally just got his bad butt to go to sleep, so don't even think about waking him up," she said while screwing her face up at me.

I wanted to see my lil' nigga, but wasn't no way in the world I was about to wake his bad ass up. I had to listen to Mom's since she was taking care of him while Olay was in California on her bullshit.

143

"Aight, I'll try and swing back later on tonight or if not, then in the morning," I said then stood up getting ready to leave. She pulled me back down by the arm, "Sit down so I can have a talk with you," she said in the same tone she'd been using since I was a child.

I already knew what time it was, so I just sat back down and accepted it. She usually didn't try and lecture me or get into my personal life, so when she did, I just chopped it up.

"Don't tell me this about Olay crying to you, Mama, cause I'm not moving to LA," I let that be known from the jump.

"You know that girl been asking me to talk to you, plus I wanna talk about a few things that's been on my mind anyways."

"What's on your mind, Mama?"

"You and these damn streets. Boy, you know exactly what. Every time I turn the News on I'm hoping it's not you that's dead. Then, when I find out it's not you that's dead, I automatically get to thinking that you're the one doing all the killing. You know I hear things about you all the time. When is enough going to be enough?" she asked, dead ass serious.

It was always the same thing with her and Olay, they wanted me to get out of the streets and be a family man. They acted like they didn't understand that this street shit was in me. That wasn't going nowhere.

"I don't know, Mama, I haven't thought about it, I've been busy," I kept it one hunnid with her.

"Well you need to start thinking about it, don't you think? In case you forgot, there are people out here that values your life, including your son."

I sighed, "I know, Mother," was all I managed to say.

"Well, act like it then," she shot back with a lil' attitude.

I laid back on the couch getting real comfortable cause I knew it was gone be awhile. "I'm listening, Mother."

"You think you're funny, huh?" she asked, then sat up straighter.

I ended up sitting there for the next hour, getting lectured about my lifestyle and slowing down with Olay. I sat there

Steady Mobbin'

nodding my head acting like I was actually thinking on what she was saying.

Marcellus Allen

Chapter 13
June 25th

It had been a few weeks since that shit at the funeral, but we definitely had the city turnt up! Those Gutta Squad niggas was slidin' a lil' bit and now they had all the Crips ridin' with them. I guess that funeral stunt was just way too disrespectful for their crippin'. Oh well, I didn't give a fuck and my niggas didn't either, they knew where to find us at.

Even though it was dry out there, I was still getting to the bag, that wasn't never gone stop. I was still slangin' thangs throughout the city, and we even opened up a few more trap houses. I had niggas coming from Seattle and Oakland to cop from me. Niggas weren't fucking with me on no money shit, period.

"You trust that nigga, Mike, blood?" Bobbie asked from the passenger seat.

"Naw, I don't trust him, but I doubt he'll never get on some funny shit. He ain't built like that," I said totally disregarding that niggas' gangsta.

We were on our way to meet Mike, so I could drop off three birds to him. He was stepping his weight up and making me more money, so I was fuckin' with him. We were definitely bumping heads with his Piru niggas, but he had been on some *'I ain't in it'* type of shit. It was always niggas that weren't in it when the beef got real, that's just how shit went.

"Yeah, blood is a bitch," he disrespected Mike's gangsta too.

"Let's just hurry up and get this money so we can get to the mall before it closes," I said then parked in the same lot on 42nd and Killingsworth as I did last time.

Mike was already waiting in his Benz when I pulled in. I parked a few spots away from him then jumped out with the work. He jumped out and met me half way, looking all nervous and shit. He kept looking around like he was expecting for the Feds to jump out at any moment. That shit must have been contagious cause next thing I knew, I had started looking around all paranoid too.

"Nigga, why you acting all nervous and shit again? You making me paranoid now!" I questioned him.

"My bad, blood, you know how hot shit been out there," he said then looked around again real fast.

I handed him the bag. "Those niggas still trippin' on you for fuckin' with me?" I asked, already knowing the answer.

He handed the bag of money over. "Man, fuck those niggas, blood. I'm focused on getting this money." He looked around again.

I walked away from him. I couldn't stand ho ass niggas, plus I was in a rush. We were too hot to be standing around politicking about some dumb shit.

I turned around right before I reached my car and the nigga was following me looking all weird and shit.

"What's poppin', you good?" I asked him.

"Oh yeah, I wanted to ask you summin' real quick," he said.

"Speak yo mind, nigga."

"You think we gone be able to squash all this shit before it goes too far?"

I opened the door and tossed the bag in the car before facing him. "It's already went too far, nigga." I gave it to him raw then jumped in the whip.

"What's up with this nigga, blood?" Bobbie asked when I got in.

I looked at the Mike as he turned around. I was about to get out and say something, but my phone started going off. I pulled it out my pocket and saw it was Moms calling. At the same time, out of the corner of my eye I saw Mike spin around with a big ass banger in his hand.

Pow! Pow! Pow!

He ran back toward us blasting through the car windows. Pow! Pow! Pow!

I dove to the floorboard, forgetting in the heat of the moment that the Maserati was bulletproof. By the time I was able to grab my burner off my waist, Bobbie had already jumped out and started shooting.

Boom! Boom! Boom! Boom!

I got up and hopped out full of adrenaline ready for a kill. I couldn't believe Mike's bitch ass tried to kill me.

Boca! Boca! Boca!

I started letting those thangs fly at his back while he tried to run from us.

Boom! Boom! Boom! Boca! Boca! Boca! Boca! Boom! Boca! Boca!

Me and Bobbie was on that nigga. Chasing his ho ass down. That nigga was fast as a muthafucka, though and once he turned the corner he was gone. Wasn't no point in shooting no more, he had shook us and I was mad as fuck.

"Fuck, blood! I'ma kill that nigga on everything I love!" I screamed then took back off to the car.

When we got back to the lot, I saw the bag of money on the ground and swooped it up with no hesitation.

"Aye, blood, his door open," Bobbie said, then jumped in his Benz before I could say anything.

I thought he was going to search the nigga car for some more money or something, but I was wrong. He closed the door then rolled the window down. "C'mon, nigga! This a free Benz!" he shouted, then skirted out the lot.

I jumped in the 'Rati' laughing like a muthafucka! I pulled into traffic just as I started hearing sirens in the distance.

Hours Later

"They don't want me to live! A hundred shots, a hundred shots. How the fuck you miss a whole hundred shots?" I screamed out with the rest of the group.

We were at the studio, deep as shit really feeling ourselves. All my niggas were there and we had a boat load of bitches hanging out with us too. It was live! Everybody had their phones out recording me and Bobbie acting a fool in the middle of the room. We had that song *100 Shots* by Young Dolph, blasting out the speakers. That's exactly how we were feeling, bulletproof, cause just like Young Dolph, we had a nigga rush the car, but it was bulletproof.

"How the fuck you miss a whole hundred shots?" I yelled with everybody again.

I was charged up fo' real, on some straight bullshit, but I loved the cameras, so I had to show out, I couldn't help it. I had a blunt in my hand, pistol on my waist in plain sight and a bulletproof vest on with no shirt. Yeah, I was on some bullshit. When the song went off, that's when I really turnt it up.

"Aight y'all listen up, I got summin' to say for everybody out there on social media and in the streets. I told y'all bitch ass niggas on my last video that the Maserati was bulletproof but y'all thought I was just playing huh?" I paused for a few seconds to let that shit sink in for a minute, then I continued. "Anyways, tell me why this bitch ass nigga call himself tryna' kill me today while I was sitting in the car. Me and Bobbie heard those shots and we didn't even flinch, dumb ass nigga! Then to top it off, the scary ass nigga ran down the street leaving the keys to his Benz in the ignition!" When I said that, everybody started laughing.

"So, if you want yo Benz back, bitch ass nigga, my dawg Bobbie wants a hundred grand in all twenties, fuck boy!" Bobbie pulled the keys out and started showing them off. "Oh, and we're definitely gonna have yo' shit in my music video I'm shooting tomorrow too, bitch ass nigga! Fuck Piru, Fuck Gutta Squad!" I yelled, getting angrier by the second. I couldn't believe the audacity of those niggas.

"Put the Young Dolph back on and keep the cameras on for a while, let these mere mortals see how we live!" I said, then got back to feeling myself.

For the next twenty minutes, all we did was dance and talk shit. Even Bobbie was half smiling and that nigga hadn't smiled since Trell got killed. Shit, that was the first time any of us had any fun since Trell's funeral. We had all been on one, just rydin' and getting to the money. We felt untouchable even though over half of the Town was now against us.

"Marshawn! Olay said to answer yo' damn phone before she ends up killing you," Falon yelled from across the room.

I knew she did that shit on purpose, tryna scare off all the groupies with her loud ass. I looked at my phone, five missed calls from the wife. I wasn't about to call her ass, I was busy.

"Tell her I'm bout to start recording and I'll tap in with her later." I walked over to Rugar. "Aight, I'm ready to drop this shit. I didn't come with a hook that I like so I'ma just lay the verse then probably talk at the end," I told him.

"Yo, I came up with a dope idea while y'all was on that Young Dolph," he said, then started clicking away on his computer.

"What you got for me?" Every time he came up with an idea, it was something heavy.

"I'ma sample Young Dolph's voice when he says, 'how the fuck you miss a whole hundred shots?' and have him say it like every four bars. Then after yo' verse ends, when you talkin', I'ma loop it for every two bars. It's gone be dope," he broke it down.

I thought about what he said for a few seconds tryna' visualize it and how it would sound. I started nodding my head, liking the sound of it the more I thought about it. Especially since I was shootin' hella shots in the song. It made perfect sense.

"Yeah I'ma fuck with it. The only thing is, I wrote this verse before they shot my car up," I told him.

"That's why you gone talk shit about it after the verse. It's gone be hard as fuck, I'm telling you," Rugar stated, convincing me.

"Aight, let's get it then." I made my way inside the booth. I scrolled through my I-Phone looking for my verse while he put the finishing touches on the beat. By the time I was done putting the rag over the microphone and finishing the rest of my ritual, he was ready to make it happen.

"Yo, O, the sample gone drop by itself then the beat gone drop, soon as you hear the beat, just start rapping," he told me.

I nodded my head, then started concentrating. Everybody had their phones pointed at me recording it was dead silent in there.

How the fuck you miss a whole hundred shots. The sample played in my headphones. Then the beat dropped, and I missed my spot.

"Yo, play it back, I fucked up," I told Rugar.

"It's good, just gotta time it right. Get ready," he replied.

I waited a few seconds until it came back in, I hated when I messed up.

How the fuck you miss a whole hundred shots! I heard and got ready. Then the beat dropped.

Fuck the candlelights, we ain't respecting they wishes/we knockin' down the pictures, portraying them dead bitches/half the town say we trippin', so they clickin' up/tell those cowards they ain't thick enough and all my niggas rich as fuck.

How the fuck you miss a whole hundred shots? Young Dolph jumped in.

"At Trell's funeral I was posted with the .45/gave 'em too much credit, I was thinking they would slide by/you know, eye for an eye, but niggas ain't got no heart/had the nerve to blame task for the reason they ain't spark/ How the fuck you miss a whole hundred shots? The sample came in.

On the phone with the Crips niggas wanna have a sit down/slide by the funeral so everybody sick now/shot that other pussy three times he just won't die/tryna' get Butta out the house, he just won't ride/How the fuck you miss a whole hundred shots/Gutta Squad chain hanging from the neck, bet they want it back/but it's sixty rounds in the Mac .90 with the shoulder strap/all red seats in the inside of the Maserati/all that blood, brings back memories of my last body.

How the fuck you miss a whole hundred shots?

"You pussy ass niggas don't want me to live right? So, that's the price of being wanted?" I said, then started laughing.

Steady Mobbin'

After the sample played, I got right back at it. "Weak ass nigga ran up on that bulletproof thang with that lil' revolver, his hand was shaking and shit, the nigga was nervous! You ain't no killer nigga! You hear me!? Huh? Bobbie got that Benz too nigga, all on Snapchat and shit with it. You niggas stop calling my phone too, hell naw we can't talk it out! Mob up or get shot down, the city's ours. Ain't nobody safe now. bitches, get it too!" I yelled that last part, as the beat went off.

Soon as I walked out, it was all hugs and handshakes, they loved it when I gassed those niggas. My phone went off and I saw that it was Olay. I answered, then walked to the back office.

What's up, baby mama?" I asked as I sat down behind my desk.

"You think you're funny, Marshawn. Where have you been?" she started complaining.

"At home, where you're supposed to be. What day you coming home?" I turned it around on her.

"I'll be there on the First, you know that. Now why you been ignoring me?"

"Cause my bitch suppose to be at home with me, that's why!" I replied feeling myself getting hot.

"We've been over this, Marshawn!" she yelled in my ear.

I hung up on her ass with no hesitation. I didn't have time for that shit. I was fighting real street wars on the daily, so having a war of words wasn't about to happen. Fuck that! I was becoming stressed out from everything that was going on around me, so the last thing I needed was extra stress.

I pushed Olay out of my thoughts and allowed the evil ones to replace her. I still couldn't believe that fuck boy Mike really tried to kill me. That shit was funny to me. The more I thought about it, the more I came to respect their lil' weak ass plan. It did make sense, since he was the only one of those niggas that would be able to get close to me, but he fucked up and now I was on their asses. It was definitely reppin' time. I couldn't wait to get my hands on them niggas.

Marcellus Allen

Next Day

"Alright, everybody take five minutes, then we'll knock this last scene out," the director told everybody that walked away.
"I'm tired as a muthafucka, blood," Burnside complained.
We were at the strip club *Mystiques*, shooting the music video for my song 'Money Must be the Reason.' That song was my strip club anthem, the bitches be going crazy when it drop in the club. The video wasn't nothing out of the ordinary, just a bunch of niggas throwing money, while the strippers were twerking. We had all the expensive alcohol and we were rocking all of our ice, real heavy. Shit, it was basically one of our regular nights out just minus the hating ass niggas.
"Nigga, tired from what? You ain't doing shit but throwing money and mugging the camera," I told that Burnside.
"I know, but still, this shit is hella time consuming," he replied.
The director came back before I could respond again.
"O-Dawg, did you still wanna shoot in the parking lot? Because if so, we can just do that right now and be done in here," he told me.
"Naw, I want the video to switch to my song 'Funeral Music' when we get to the lot, I want this whole song in here."
"Okay, well let's get started then. Everybody back to their positions!" he yelled, and everybody started getting ready.
I went and sat on the couch in the VIP section, while this thick stripper started grinding on me. I got to tossing hundreds while my niggas were standing on the couch, spilling alcohol and throwing gang signs. We finished that last scene in under ten minutes then took the show outside.
"So, this is how I want it to look," I said to the director as we were looking around tryna' get it right. "We gone line all of our cars up in a circle but have the Maserati and the Benz facing each other in the middle. Bobbie gone be standing on the Benz while I'm rapping and everybody else gone be standing around

154

me doing whatever they feel like doing. I want this video to be real grimmey, real street shit, aight?"

"Yeah, I got you, and I'ma add some stuff to the video when it's done. Have it go black and white for a few bars then back to color, then mix it up. I know exactly what you want." He started rubbing his hands together and nodding his head, really getting into it.

"Yeah, that sounds gucci, let me get everybody ready," I told him, then walked over to my niggas who were macking on the strippers. "Y'all put all the cars in a circle. Just like we talked about it. it's time."

"O-Dawg, can we be in this video too?" the stripper that was grinding on me the whole time asked.

Boc! Boc! Boc! Boc! Boc!

The sound of gunfire interrupted our conversation, making everybody get low to the ground.

"Fuck the Mob!" somebody yelled out.

By the time I grabbed my burner and jumped up, all I could see was a black car speeding through the traffic. We were dealing with ho niggas!

"Them niggas ain't tryna' hit nobody. It's thirty muthafuckaz out here and ain't nobody grazed. Everybody get back in position. Yo, Scott, get ready to start directing!" I told my niggas, then yelled at the director.

"Yo O, you know gang task about to use that for a reason to come shut us down," Gotti said.

"Fuck the pigs, son, we staying out here," Jersey Joe said, before I could respond.

I wanted to stay and finish my video bad as a muthafucka, my pride and ego were eating me up. I couldn't wait to drop that diss song on them bitch ass niggas.

"I know where we can go film the video and it's better than here," Burnside spoke up.

"Where?" I asked.

"The parking garage downtown across the street from the Justice Center," he said.

I thought about what he said and started visualizing it. It was perfect. The roof up there was always empty and isolated, and we wouldn't have to worry about the pigs.

"You talking about on the roof top?" I asked.

"Exactly!" he answered.

"Yo, Scott, I'ma shoot you an extra five hundred to move everything over there. That's gucci?" I asked the director.

"Cool with me," he said.

"Aight, c'mon everybody, shoot downtown," I said, then hurried up and jumped in the whip before faggot ass gang task showed up.

Thirty minutes later, we were on the roof top and almost ready to start shooting the video. I should have thought of that place in the first place. It was low-key as hell. The hot as summer time sun felt like it was right on top of our heads. We were at least fifteen stories up and it felt like it got fifty degrees hotter on me!

I took my hoody off and didn't have no top on except my bulletproof vest, and of course my iced-out Jesus piece. Since we were isolated up there, I decided to turn things up for the video. I grabbed the AK-47 from out my trunk and let it hang from the strap around my shoulder. As soon as my niggas saw what type of time I was on, they got to grabbing smacks from everywhere. Them niggas couldn't wait to start flashing those guns on camera.

"Nigga, I'm bout to put my mask on, fuck that," Gotti said, then really put on one of those scary ass Halloween masks.

After I watched a few more of my niggas put masks on, that's when I decided that's how I wanted my whole video. Masks on, guns out.

"Yo, I want everybody to cover their faces up except Bobbie. We gone be the only ones with our face showing. I want everybody standing in front of a car inside the circle. I'ma walk around rapping. When the camera is on you, you can do whatever it is you wanna do," I told everybody.

Steady Mobbin'

"I'm not feeling that mask shit, son, I ain't got nothing to hide. I'm going bare face just like y'all niggas, word is bond. You and Bobbie ain't the only niggas they want," Jersey Joe said, sounding dumb as fuck and really starting to irritate me.

That nigga was always on some bullshit, wanting to poke his chest out an out shine everybody. *This nigga probably just doing this shit cause Bobbie ain't wearing no mask,* I thought. He was so caught up in his ego contest, that he missed the whole concept of the video. I damn sho wasn't about to explain myself or kiss no nigga's ass.

"Blood, I'm not about to stand here in this hot ass sun explaining myself to you. If you tryna' be in the video than put the mask on, if not then that's on you," I told that nigga, then stood in the circle and waited for the director to get ready.

How the fuck you miss a whole hundred shots.

The rest of the video shoot went by with no other problems and came out exactly how I wanted it to. We laid it on thick as a muthafucka the whole video; guns, cars, jewelry and gang signs. I knew when them bitch ass niggas saw that video, they would be sick to their stomachs. I was really rubbing it in on those pussies.

Bobbie standing on that ho nigga's Benz just made the video ten times funnier and more street. Those niggas could say whatever they wanted on the internet, we were winning on the scoreboard. I was smiling on the outside and having fun diggin' in those pussy's chests, but I was boiling inside. They tried to kill me, and I never took that shit lightly. They must have felt like they couldn't be touched. Well, I was about to put my hands on them. I couldn't wait. The war was officially on with the Pirus.

Marcellus Allen

Chapter 14
June 30, 2017

Moment of silence, this for the rivals/I pray that you die on the bible/dem choppaz don't spin in the spiral, they hit summin' vital/and that was for diamond/poverty stricken my trenches is slimy/they bring up my demons, why must you remind me?

Mozzy's verse thumping out of the stereo was like the soundtrack to my heart at that moment. I was sitting in the backseat of Burnside's porch truck mad as a muthafucka. I had on black sweats, black hoody and a pair of black gloves on. It was a lil' after five o'clock in the evening, so the sun was starting to lose some of its heat, but the twin .40 cal's in my hoody were about to heat shit back up.

I'ma kill these niggas, I said to myself as I gripped both of my pistols.

"Yo, son, who you think it was? Gutta Squad or Piru?" Jersey Joe asked Burnside from the passenger's seat.

"Ain't no telling, but we gone find out when we get there," he replied.

I knew exactly who did it. I could tell by how they did it. They let the lil' niggas live, that's all I needed to know. I wasn't expecting what happened though. I wondered if they prepared for what was to happen next. That's the only thing I was really thinking about, what was their angle? I knew after that video dropped that something was gone happen, but they had just fucked up.

When we pulled up to the trap house on 10th and Skidmore Street, the first thing I noticed was how dry the block was. *Fuckin' ghost town,* I thought as we climbed the steps. Realizing how much money I was losing at that moment made me ten times madder. I gripped my guns again while Burnside knocked on the door.

The door flew open and a lil nigga named Phatz was standing there with a 12 gauge in his hand. I saw the look of concern written all over his face.

159

"Nigga, if you woulda' been on point like this in the first place, we wouldn't be here right now, son, so cut the crap and move out the way." Joe pulled his card.

He looked Joe dead in the eyes. The concern was gone but the anger was visible. He looked at Burnside then at me for a quick second before he walked in the spot and stood in the corner. *He doesn't recognize me,* I told myself then walked in. I had my hood covering most of my face, plus I wasn't wearing my glasses, exactly what I wanted.

Lil Bobby was standing up against the wall, too, when we walked in. I could read what he was thinking. I sat down on the couch while everybody else stood. I wanted to see how everything would unfold. It had been a while since I had actually been hands on with a trap house problem.

This wasn't no regular trap house problem, though. I lost eighty-thousand and over a brick of hard, that shit was personal.

"Why you still got that gauge in yo hand, nigga?" Burnside asked, leaving no doubt that he felt some type of way.

Phatz looked down at the gun like he was noticing it for the first time. "Oh, my bad," he said then tossed it on the floor.

Joe walked over and picked the gun up keeping eye contact with him the whole time. The tension was thick in the room, but I was far from worried about it.

"What about you, nigga, where yo' heat at?" Burnside turned his attention to Lil' Bobby.

"Right here," he responded, then handed his gun to Joe.

It took everything in me not to start laughing in their faces. They had fucked up on so many levels from the time we knocked on the door, that I was actually convinced they had nothing to do with the robbery. They had heart, but they damn sho didn't mastermind no robbery against me.

"Aight, tell me what happened last night. Don't leave nothing out 'cause it can cost y'all lives," Burnside demanded folding his arms and mugging them down.

After ten minutes of listening to their version of the story, with Burnside poking holes through it, I knew exactly what happened. I was definitely mad as fuck, but I could relate to it. When I was younger I was in charge of a trap house before.

"Phatz, what's the bitch name?" I finally spoke up for the first time.

He looked over at me like I was crazy.

"Nigga, who is you? I never said nothin' about no bitch." He came at me real aggressively.

Before I could blink my eyes, Joe had his pistol aimed right at his face. "Say summin' else, son," he growled.

I jumped off the couch, took my hood off and walked up in Phat face. He knew at that instance that he had made a deadly mistake and by the look of his homie, he knew too. I eased Joe's arm down real slow while keeping eye contact with Phatz.

You know who I am now?" I asked real calm like. Phat nodded his head. "What about you?" I asked Lil Bobby. He nodded as well.

"Yo, son, let's just kill these niggas," said Joe.

"You wanna know the three reasons why I'm not gone kill you and ya man's?" I asked Phatz.

He swallowed hard then said, "Yeah."

"Because you must be a good nigga for ya man's over here to be willing to die for you over some pussy." They looked at each other, then back at me, as I continued. "Secondly, I've been young, dumb and horny before, so trust me when I tell you I know exactly what happened in here. Third, Phatz you're going to tell me that bitch's name, 'cause she the one set y'all up."

"Why you think--"

"'Cause you've been the aggressive one since we got here, which means it was yo' bitch," I cut him off. "Lil' Bobby just been standing here out of loyalty. Why I think she set you up? Cause you niggas still alive, that's why. She got seduced or forced out of loyalty to set this up, but she didn't want you dead, and that's how I know it was those Murda Squad niggas. The crab woulda killed both of y'all, especially Pull-Out. I guarantee she got family from there or it's her best friend family, some shit like that. You were back there getting ya dick sucked and they came right in here huh?" I broke it down.

"Yeah, that's what happened, O-Dawg, I'm sorry, blood, let me make it right," Phatz finally confessed.

"Let's kill this nigga, blood. I don't trust this him, word is bond." Joe was on one.

"Fuck you, nigga, you keep saying that shit. I'ma make you pull that trigga." Phatz looked Joe dead in his eyes.

"Oh, these niggas got heart," Burnside said, finding the situation half way funny.

"Yeah, Bobbie know how to pick 'em." Joe was being sarcastic.

So that's where the extra animosity is coming from, I said to myself. It was the trap house that Bobbie was in charge of, but he was in Seattle on business, so he had to handle it. I really didn't even know those lil niggas like that, but I knew of them. Bobbie was grooming those them, so I wanted to at least respect that fact.

"Call the bitch on speaker phone and tell her you need to link up with her," I said.

Phatz hesitated a lil' bit then pulled his phone out.

"I lost a lot of money and dope, my nigga, don't play with me right now," I warned.

He called her a few times, but kept getting sent to voice mail. I could see the anger in his eyes at that point. He knew. I handed over my phone without saying a word, she answered on the first try.

"Hello?"

"Katrina? Why the fuck you weren't answering my calls?" Phatz asked, now he was really mad.

"Because I'm busy right now, that's why. What's so important that you had to call from a different number?"

"I need to holla at you about some shit in person, like ASAP."

"Well, I'm busy tonight."

"Aight, we'll link up tomorrow," he compromised.

162

"Uhhh, I'm busy tomorrow too."

He sighed loudly, "Then, when the fuck you wanna meet up? You acting real weird right now," he said, finally losing his temper.

"I don't know, I'm just real busy this week. I'll let you know when." She sounded irritated.

It was clear that she was lying and guilty about something.I was done listening to her play games. I took the phone from him.

"Yo, Katrina," I said, real calm like.

"Who the fuck is this?" She turnt up on me.

"This is O-Dawg, I'm sure you know exactly who I am," I paused to let my name sink in. "You made a fatal mistake by listening to those niggas, baby girl. You tell them I said I don't want the money, I want their lives. We gone see y'all real soon." I hung up before she could start lying to me. I looked at those lil' niggas real hard and slow before I told them my decision.

"I wanna see a whole bunch of R.I.P. Katrina's on Facebook this week."

I looked their asses up and down looking for any sign of weakness, or if they thought I was playing.

"We on it," Lil' Bobby spoke up.

I stared in Phatz eyes waiting for him to acknowledge what the fuck I said.

"We on it," he gave in, after probably contemplating his options.

"I'm not gone put y'all in debt for all the shit that was lost." I saw them breathe a sigh of relief as soon as they heard those words. "But y'all do owe me, so this is what I want. After that bitch is dead, I want y'all to body one of those Piru niggas for runnin' in here. Then body one of those Squad niggas, we clear?"

"We clear," they said at the same time.

"I was young once too, but don't fuck up like this again." I gave them that final warning, then walked out the house.

Marcellus Allen

We didn't even get off the block for two full minutes before Joe turned around in his seat and started bitching.

"Son, I can't believe you let those niggas off the hook that easy. You should of a least let me shoot em in the legs, word is bond. Yo, back home those niggas would of got thrown off the roof top or summin', real shit."

"They not getting off easy," I said, not feeling like explaining myself.

"Shit, I'ma steal eight bands then, son, and just let me catch a body and we call it even," he relied on a snide tone.

"Nigga, stop counting my muthafuckin' money and just play yo' part. I know how to run my shit. In case you forgot, I touched a million dollars before I met you, blood!"

Burnside gone have to talk to this nigga or send 'em back home before I kill 'em. That's what ran through my mind.

That was my first time talking to him like that, but I should have been done it. He was really starting to wear down my patience at that point and I knew I had been more than patient with him. He had been a good nigga on every level, but his mouth was getting out of hand. I could see what Bobbie had been talking about. That nigga didn't know when to shut the fuck up.

"So, what's the verdict for the night? Are you ridin' or are we gonna wait for another time." Burnside jumped in.

"I'm tryna' murk summin' tonight, son. I need to release some tension," Joe said, not surprising either one of us.

"Take me to all of our main trap spots so I can check up on shit, personally. It's been too long since I've done that. We need to prepare everybody, then we ridin' out," I said then leaned back.

By the time we got through checking on all the trap spots, the sun had gone completely down, but the tension was still thick. Hitting up all those spots ended up being more irritating then anything. Joe found something to complain about in every spot and to keep it real he had a lot of valid points.

164

Steady Mobbin'

I'ma holla at Bobbie and Gotti about this shit tomorrow. I promised myself as we drove with murder on our minds.

We drove past the corner store on 17th and Killingsworth and saw a couple of niggas walking inside the store. I couldn't see their faces but that didn't matter cause only those Piru niggas hung out there, especially at night.

"There them niggas go right there, blood," Burnside got all excited.

"Bend the block then park right across the street," I said then pulled the .40's out of my hoody.

I had it on my mind that as soon as they came out the store, we were jumping out and slumping them in the parking lot.

"Here they come, son," Joe said.

Soon as the words left his mouth, my feet were touching the pavement. Take a deep breath, I know what I'm doing, I said to calm myself. Right before I got ready to aim my heats, I looked in those niggas faces and couldn't recognize any of them. They looked like a couple of teenagers rocking those weird ass haircuts and tight ass clothes.

I saw it in their eyes, they weren't no street niggas. They stood there frozen, not knowing what to do.

"Hold up, they just some kids," I said blocking Joe, with my arm, from crossing the street.

"Fuck, son!"

We jumped back in the car and roamed their hood for another five minutes not finding anybody. It was like a ghost town out there, but we were far from done.

"It seems like every time a nigga try and slide through they hood, they be in the house hiding and shit. They know what time it is," Burnside pounded the steering wheel.

"Don't get all worked up for nothing, nigga, keep ya head. Slide by 87th and Flavel. We bout to fuck they trap spot up. I heard they been getting money out that way too," I said, then leaned back trying to ease my mind and get prepared.

When we got there twenty minutes later, it was live out there just like I expected. It wasn't hard to find the right house, we just followed the fiends.

"Drive real slow so we can get a good lay out of the land. Joe, see if you can find a look out house cause that's the last thing we need right now," I coached, as we rolled down the street looking around.

They had a nice little operation going on out there, but we were about to shake some shit up. It was a lot of base heads out there and three niggas by my count that was slangin'. We sat parked for a few minutes just watching how everything went down. One time one of the niggas knocked on the door and had a re-up real quick. I got a quick glance, but all I could make out was one nigga standing in the front room.

"This shit gone be easy. I'm ready whenever y'all is," Burnside said, but turned around looking at me.

Take a deep breath. I know what I'm doing, I said to myself.

I pulled my hood over my head then bounced out without saying a single word. Wasn't nothing to talk about. We knew what we came for. Crack heads got spider senses or some shit because they always knew when it was about to be some shit. The one that was buying his dope, turned his head and looked right at us, then took off running.

The nigga that was serving him looked at us like he had just seen a ghost, then reached for his waist. Our cover was blown.

"What's up now, niggas!" I yelled, then lifted my guns.

Boom! Boom! Boom! Boom! Boom! Boom! Boom! Boc! Boc! Boc!

We filled that nigga chest up and his back, as he tried to run. He died with his gun on his waist. What a pussy. Crack heads started running off the block for dear life and those other niggas found some heart.

Boom! Boom! Boom! Boom! Boom! Boc! Boc! Boca! Boca! Boca! Boca!

We were in a full fledge shootout now, and that's exactly how I liked it. Burnside and Joe ran in the middle of the street shooting while I stayed on the sidewalk. Another one of them came running down the street bustin' at us from nowhere. I guess he was the brave heart type. I liked it.

Boc! Boc! Boc! Boc! Boc! Boc! Boc! Boc! Boom! Boom! Boom! Boca! Boca!

One of those pussies tried to run and duck down behind another car and got flatlined by Burnside.

Boc! Boc! Boc!

He dropped like a fly, right in the street. It seemed like his pistol slid across the street in slow motion.

"Y'all niggas know whose block y'all fuckin' with?" One of them yelled from behind a car, then shot at Joe.

Boc! Boc!

I hated when niggas asked dumb ass questions like that. At this point, what did it matter? The gun shots had already started, so it wasn't like niggas were about to pack up and leave. We came to kill niggas.

"Naw, son, why don't you come over here and tell us!" Joe mocked him.

Boom! Boom! Boom! Boom!

Soon as Joe started eating the car up, the other nigga made a dash for the house. I took after that nigga figuring those two could handle the pussy behind the car.

Boom! Boom! Boom! Boom! Boom!

I started sending that hot shit his way while I chased him down. Unn-unn, don't run now, nigga, I said like he could hear me.

Soon as he got to the bottom of the stairs he decided to let his nuts hang a lil' bit.

Boc! Boc! Boc! Boc! Boc!

He turned around and started gassing me! I had to duck behind a car real quick.

Boca! Boca! Boca! Boc! Boc! Boc! Boc! Boca!

I heard the shots going off in the distance and knew what that meant, man down. That shit got me pumped up! I came from behind that car on some ready to die shit and saw that pussy trying to make it up the stairs.

Boom! Boom! Boom! Boom! Boom! Boom!

"Aghh!" he screamed out.

That's yo ass, boy. I watched him try and climb the last few steps. Soon as he crawled on the porch I was right there standing over him, looking like the devil.

"C'mon, blood, don't kill me," he pleaded for his life, looking for mercy in my eyes. But he found none.

"Oh, now we bloods, huh? You looking for some damn love? Here."

Boom! Boom! Boom!

I filled his chest up, silencing him forever. Now he can go to blood heaven, I told myself, then knocked on the door.

Knock! Knock! Knock!

I pounded harder and harder. "I just wanna talk to you," I teased him.

"You come through that door and I guarantee we ain't doing no talkin'!" he yelled out.

I moved to the side of the door just in case that nigga started bustin' through the door. A scary muthafucka would do anything.

"Tell yo weak ass big homie that shit he stole from us came with a price tag and we coming to collect. Tell 'em we ain't coming for his money, we coming for his life," I said, and then I took off for the car.

We were just getting warmed up. I had something real nice brewing for those niggas.

Steady Mobbin'

Chapter 15

The next morning, I was staring in the mirror while brushing my teeth, trying to read myself. My eyes were pitch black. My baby face was still intact, but my eyes gave me away. I looked like a fuckin' demon. The last few months had really worn my soul down, but it was better than the grave yard.

I leaned in closer to the mirror so I could really peek deep into my eyes. Yeah, I was losing my soul, I thought as I leaned back. *But, at least I'm rich bitch,* I said to myself.

"Don't be taking forever, Tamia!" I yelled knowing damn well she would.

I picked up my .45 from off the counter and stared at it for a minute. I had never used it before. It was fresh out the box. I had to dump the .40's in the river the night before. I wondered how long the new banger was going to last. Just then, my phone started ringing, snapping me out my zone.

"I don't recognize this number, so speak fast," I answered with an attitude.

"This Big Smoke, what's brackin?"

Big Smoke was one of the first Bloods to come down to Portland from Compton. Him and his West Side Piru homies were the ones responsible for the first Blood sets in the Town, most of them. He'd been on some fall back shit for years, just stacking his money and pushing that Damu unity. With that being said, I had got a felling what this call was about soon as he said his name.

"Shit, just steady mobbin', the usual, what's brackin' though?" I asked, already knowing.

"I wanna have a sit down, before things get outta hand with you and the homie," he said.

The homie, huh? I wondered.

"Who you talkin' about? Bitch ass Floyd? That nigga a dead man walking, blood, I ain't even gone lie to you. He done crossed a line that can't be re-drawn, so tell his ho ass to stop calling you tryna' get you to play Farrakhan. Tell his punk ass to come get this *work!*"

"He ain't call me, I'm reaching out to both of y'all niggas personally. It's a lot of money being jeopardized by this situation that you don't know about. I'm asking that out of respect you agree to at least have a sit down, then we go from there," he explained, sounding irritated.

Tamia came and wrapped her arms around me, then kissed me on the neck. That reminded me I had better shit to be doing with my time. I had to get to the bag.

"Aight, we can do that, outta respect for you. I'm in the middle of something right now though, so just hit me up when you got the details and tell that bitch ass nigga I'm not letting off the gas either, in the meantime."

After I hung up, I turned around and noticed that Tamia wasn't dressed yet. "Mia, come on, baby, finish getting dressed," I pleaded.

"I'm more dressed than you." She looked me up and down. "I gotta talk to you about two things before we leave, Papi."

Aww shit, she said Papi, I warned myself, then walked out of the bathroom. She only spoke that Spanish shit when we were fuckin'. *She either wants some money or shit is about to get real.* I just knew it was the latter.

"We bout to go drop off five bricks and you wanna have a talk? What kinda of shit is you on?" I asked, while I sat on the bed putting my clothes on.

She stood in front of me with her hand on her hip tryna look all serious.

"Come on and spit it out so we can go and take care of this business, Tamia." Frustration was beginning to set in with me.

"So, if that other bitch gets back in town today, what does that mean? You not gone be here no more?" she asked, already knowing the answer.

I had forgotten what day it was. She must have had it marked on her calendar or something.

"Whenever Olay comes back, then yes, shit will go back to normal. You already know that. Please don't start a frivolous argument right now. Damn!"

I gave it to her raw, not fully understanding why she felt the need to ask a dumb ass question. She stood there looking stupid, not saying anything, while I finished getting dressed. I was trying not to flash on her bipolar ass for not getting dressed, but I knew that's what she wanted me to do.

"What's the second thing you wanted to talk to me about? 'Cause obviously you got some shit to get off yo' chest before you get dressed. So, give it to me raw," I told her as I stepped up to the mirror to check myself out.

I had on some 501 jeans, peanut butter Timbaland boots, and a True Religion hoody to match. Ever since I started wearing that vest every day, I had to either wear a hoody or some kind of jacket. That shit had me burning up in that summer heat, but I kept telling my paranoid self, I'd rather deal with the burning sun than a burning bullet. Fuck that.

"I'm pregnant!" she blurted out.

I turned around and stared right through her ass. I knew she was telling the truth from the moment the words left her mouth. *Now, I really done fucked up,* I chastised myself. I instantly got sick to my stomach, because I knew Olay was gone flip the fuck out. She had forgiven me for a lot of shit, but I doubted this was going to be added to the list. *She gon leave my ass after this come out,* the voice in my head said.

All types of crazy thoughts started running through my head. I thought about punching Tamia dead in the stomach, but quickly dismissed that retarded shit. I thought about shooting her too, then threw that idea out the window. I even thought about paying one of my home girls to ambush her and stomp the baby out, then decided that was foul too. I needed more time to figure shit out, and at that moment, my mind was focused on securing the bag.

Baby girl read me like a muthafuckin open book. "I'm not getting no abortion either, nigga, so you might as well get that out yo' head. You got me highly fucked up. I'm not killing my baby, so you gone have to kill me first, and don't think you about to abandon us either, 'cause I'll kill yo' ass and you know I'm not playing with you, Marshawn!" she threatened me, her voice getting louder and louder.

If she only knew what I had really been thinking.

"Bitch, shut the fuck up," I growled at her, then got right up in her face. It took everything in me not to slap her ass. "Keep talkin' that gangsta shit to me and see what happens. You ain't calling no shots around here, so shut the fuck up before I force you to lose the baby. Don't let that pregnant shit go to yo' head. Now, finish getting dressed so we can go get this money. We'll talk about the baby later on." I left the room before my demons kicked in.

I sat on the couch smoking a blunt tryna' calm my nerves before I went ape shit. I knew it wasn't her fault she got pregnant, but I wasn't feeling how she came at me, like I was a sucka' or summin'. The whole time Olay was gone, I had been at Tamia's spot playing house and shit. I was bustin' nuts in her ass every single day knowing I was out of pocket.

I'ma have to convince her to get an abortion.

She came out thirty minutes later looking bad as a muthafucka. I ain't even gone lie. She had on a skirt that hugged her curves, a blouse and some expensive ass heels, I know I had to have paid for. Plus, she had her long ass hair flowing straight down just the way I liked it. *She knows what she's doing,* I said to myself. I felt like fuckin' her right then and there, but she walked right outside.

It took us twenty minutes to get to the Olive Garden but when we did, I felt relieved. It was bad enough that I had five bricks stuffed in Tamia's bag, but it made it worse with all the tension in the air. We didn't say nothing to each other the whole car ride. I caught her giving me the side eye a couple times, but I just kept on listening to Kevin Gates, ignoring her.

Steady Mobbin'

When we parked, it was time to switch to business mode and I was hoping she was ready.

"Listen, Mia, we're leaving all personal shit inside this car. When we step out, I'ma need for you…"

She cut me off. "Nigga, I know what I need to do, so save the lectures for that square bitch you got," she said with contempt.

I felt the fire burning up inside of me. It took extreme patience not to slap her ass. I grabbed her by the chin and turned her face so that she was looking directly in my eyes.

"I'm trying real hard not to slap the fuck out of you, blood, stop testing me. You know I don't go for that smart mouth shit!"

I held her stare for a few seconds, then let her go. I calmed myself down while she fixed her makeup in the mirror. After I knew I was good, I jumped out, then went and opened her door like the perfect gentleman on a date.

I found my nigga Flash and his girl sitting in the back by the windows overlooking the parking lot. Flash was the main nigga from the Bay area that I hit off with bricks on a regular. He was a real stand up nigga that busted his gun, but was also about his paper. Him and his crew was always down here getting money and networking. I fucked with him hard.

After I hugged his girl, Melissa, who he always brought with him on our deals, I dapped him up, then sat down.

"What's mobbin', my nigga? I see you shining and shit. I see you!" I commented on his jewels, just making small talk.

"Naw, nigga, I see *you*. They told me you was ridin' round in a bulletproof Maserati and now I see for myself." He looked out the window with a smile on his face.

I smirked. "That's the price for being wanted, you know how that go. What's new though?"

"Dawg, I've been buying up all the lean down here and I'm 'bout to make a killin' back home. I've been payin' niggas to break in the stores at night and snatch the ingredients I need for the lean. This shit crazy, bruh, they keep that shit locked up like a prison back home," he said shocked.

"That's cause Portland niggas is always jumping on shit late, but once them crackers get wind to what's going on, they'll shut down shop."

"Well, I'ma get this money till they do."

The waiter came over and took our orders, then we just chopped it up about music and sports for the next twenty minutes until the women went to the bathroom. As soon as they left, Flash's whole facial expression changed as he leaned closer over the table.

"Say, bruh, word just came across the wire that it's a bounty on yo' head for twenty stacks," he told me, I could hear the concern in his voice.

I was a lil' surprised, but not shocked at his revelation. I actually found the shit real amusing to tell the truth. Right then and there I decided the fates of many. I couldn't wait to get that new .45 dirty. It was burning a hole through my waist, but I played it cool.

"Twenty bands, huh? I'm insulted, I got that on me right now," I laughed. "Let me guess, it came from my own blood niggas, huh?" I already knew the answer.

"Yeah, bruh, and they approached my peoples about it, but I put a stop to that shit," he assured me.

"Good looking. I appreciate it." I steepled my hands under my chin like I was in deep thought.

"This what I'ma do 'cause I know yo' peoples is hungry and I believe in feeding the wolves. I'ma double the amount on that bitch nigga. Forty bands for Floyd's bitch ass and twenty for any hit of top niggas. How that sound?"

I really didn't agree with putting hits on niggas, I always felt like that was some sucka' shit, but I did it cause I considered myself a chess player and that was a power move. I knew those Oakland boys wanted to collect the twenty bands, even though they would have gone home in a pine box fuckin' with me, but that was unnecessary. Why go through all of that when I could use them to my advantage to apply pressure? Now, they were the hunted.

174

"Bruh, it sounds like the wolves are about to be licking their chops," he said, then we both burst out laughing.

The women returned shortly after and we finished our meals and talked shit until it was time to leave.

"Everything go good, baby?" I asked, as I drove off the lot.

"We good," she answered, then picked the oversized bag up showing me all the money inside.

I pulled up to my house a few hours later and the first thing I noticed was Falon's truck parked in the driveway. *Aww shit, time to deal with these crazy ass bitches,* I said to myself. Soon as I stepped inside, my stomach growled as my nose took in all the different aromas emanating from the kitchen.

"What y'all in there cooking?" I yelled out, then took my shoes off and tossed my gun on the table.

"What's up, sucka?" Falon came out and gave me a quick hug.

"Is she trippin?" I whispered, tryna figure out how I was gone play it.

"Baby!" Olay came out yelling, giving me my answer.

She ran over and jumped on me, wrapped her legs around my waist and stuck her tongue in my mouth. I palmed her ass like a real nigga and got to tonguing her back. I didn't realize how much I missed my bitch until that very moment. Just holding her like that felt like the best feeling in the world. I didn't love nobody more than I loved that girl.

"Damn, go get a room," Falon said.

"We got five, now take yo' hating ass home, cause we got shit to do," I said, then placed wifey on the ground.

"Boy, I've been kicked outta better places than this," Falon cracked.

"What hotel was that?" I shot back.

She started laughing, then flipped me off. "Fuck you, nigga," she grabbed her purse and put her heels on.

"Thanks for helping me cook, sis," Olay said.

"You're welcome, and when you take his dick out ya mouth, don't call me cause I'll probably have Joe's in mine. Bye, bitch."

"Bye, ratchet ass," Olay replied.

"I thought you chose Bobbie?" I said then looked her up and down like she was crazy.

"I ain't decided yet. Stop counting my dicks, nigga," she shot back, giving me that 'you don't wanna play the snitch game with me' look.

When she saw that I understood her lil' weak ass subliminal threat she hugged Olay, then walked out the door. *I'm on her head now,* I told myself as I locked the door.

"You can deal with that later, right now you need to deal with this," Olay said, then took off the boy shorts she was wearing.

My dick tried to rip through my jeans as I stared at that shaved pussy that I loved so much.

"I'm about to fuck the shit out of you," I told her, while I was rushing out of my clothes.

"Oh, I know you are." She took off her t-shirt and stood butt ass naked watching me undress.

"Leave that vest on, it gets my pussy wet," she added, right when I was taking it off.

She dropped to her knees and started licking the sides of my meat real slow, like she was trying to savor the taste of it. She made sure she licked my balls, then stuck them in her mouth, keeping eye contact the whole time.

"Put this shit in yo' mouth," I demanded. I was tryna' feel that throat.

She spit on the head then stuffed the whole dick down her throat, then pulled it all the way out. She smiled at me, then stuffed it back in, but left it there this time.

"Ahh shit," I moaned, grabbing the back of her head.

That's when she started going to work on me. She started bobbing back and forth real fast while jacking me off with one hand. That shit felt amazing.

Sluurrpp! Sluurrpp! The faster she slurped, the louder it got. Hell, just the sound of it had me ready to bust in her mouth. I gripped both sides of her head and got to face fucking her. She held on to my hips and took the dick like a real bitch.

I felt myself getting ready to blast off and had to pull out before it was too late. Usually I would have come in her mouth, but with all the fuckin' me and Tamia had been doing, I didn't know how many I had in me.

"Get up so I can taste that pussy," I told her, then lifted her up.

"We can do that later, I need some dick right now!" She spun around slow then bent over and grabbed her ankles.

Her pussy was wet as hell and winking at me, I slid right in, like I was supposed to do. "Got damn I miss that pussy," I moaned out, picking up the speed and trying not to nut.

"Ohh, ohh. She missed you," she moaned damn near yelling.

Our rhythm picked up as I got to long stroking her with my hand on the small of her back. That tight ass pussy was feeling too good.

"Umm-umm, fuck me, daddy. Pound me out," she pleaded in ecstasy, causing my dick to get even harder.

I stuck my thumb in her ass and started giving her short powerful strokes. Smack! I slapped her on the ass while digging her out.

"I'm cumming!"

That was music to my ears, 'cause I was ready to nut too. I grabbed both sides of her ass and went wild, fast as I could. She was moaning out non-stop some shit I couldn't understand.

"Whose pussy is this, bitch?" I growled, then slapped her ass again.

"It's your pussy, daddy!" she screamed.

I hit her with a few more power strokes then shot all inside of her. "Aghh!" I roared, feeling like I had just drained all of my energy inside of her pussy.

I slapped her ass one last good time then flopped down on the couch exhausted.

"Damn, baby, that was exactly what I needed. I'ma go get your plate for you," she said, then disappeared into the kitchen.

I sat there thinking to myself how I had a bad bitch that loved me to death and was loyal. I took her v-card so ain't no other nigga had my pussy. She was 100% my bitch from the jump. She was a square, had a good career and was a great mother to our son. Yet I fucked other bitches behind her back. *It's the animal in me,* I told myself, seeking justification.

"Here, baby." She placed my plate down on the table then sat down to watch me eat.

"I love you, baby, thank you," I said.

She smiled at me. "You're welcome, daddy. Hurry up and eat so we can go get it in the shower, and I need my pussy licked, real bad," she purred.

Aww shit, I'm bout to eat real slow, I thought, then started chewing even slower.

Steady Mobbin'

Chapter 16
4th of July

"Olay gone kill yo' ass, blood. You dumb as fuck," Bleed told me, stating the obvious.

We were on our way to the barber shop to get cut up, so we could be fresh for the holiday. I had decided to tell him that Tamia was pregnant.

"I know, that's why I haven't left the house since she been back. I been in there kissing her ass and rubbing her feet, tryna' make her fall in love again," I said.

That nigga started laughing, but I was dead serious. I didn't know what else to do.

"That shit ain't about to work, nigga. She Black! She bout to kick yo' ass out and that's when I'ma move in. I'ma catch her when she vulnerable with her fine ass. On Bloods, I know she got some juice." He busted out laughing again.

He thought the shit was a joke, so I turned the music up, until we pulled up to the shop. When we walked in, Bobbie was sitting in the chair already and the other one's were taken, so we had to wait.

"Yo, Billy, let me get next," I told the old school barber that was cutting Bobbie.

"You got that, young blood," he replied.

I looked around for any familiar faces and I didn't see none in the half-packed shop. Just a couple old heads getting their sons cut up and some teenagers with some weird ass hairstyles. It was hot as hell in there with the sun beaming right through the windows on us. I thought about taking my hoody off, but remembered I had that damn vest on.

"Aye, nigga, you need to talk to ya man's before I beat on 'em, real talk," Bobbie said. I already had a feeling who he was talking about.

"Who you talking about now? I asked.

179

Marcellus Allen

"Yo Jersey nigga. You know who I'm talkin' about. That nigga starting to get outta hand with this bitch. I'm 'bout to check 'em," he spat sounding dead serious.

Awww shit, here we go, I thought.

"What's the verdict now?" I asked, not feeling the whole situation at all. Niggas loved to beef over bitches and I never understood why.

"Blood, this nigga been speaking on me like a muthafucka to that bitch. I was reading the bitches text messages and he was going in." I could sense him getting angrier by the moment.

"Ahh, this nigga going through the bitches' texts. What type of sucka for love shit you on?" Bleed jumped in, laughing.

That's what I was wondering.

"'Cause, nigga, I check all my bitch's texts and call logs. If the bitch knows where I live or be spending time with me, on bloods, I'm going through it all. Ain't no bitch ever gone be able to set me up or play both sides of the fence, fuck that!" he replied, making sense like a muthafucka.

"Yeah, whatever, nigga, just get to the good parts," Bleed waved him off.

"Like I was sayin', the nigga is a straight hater. I'm starting to think it runs deeper than this bitch. He telling her, 'that nigga ain't shit,' he living off of O-Dawg's fame' and all type of other hating ass shit. Summin' ain't right with this nigga. I'm tellin' you, O," he made his case.

You reading into it way too deep, I thought but kept that to myself.

"It's just time we all have a sit down like men, then you'll realize it ain't nothing to it," I replied. "The usual, one and a half," I told the barber, as he put the cape on me.

I seen a lil' nigga get out of the waiting chair and walk out in a rush. Guess he was next, I thought to myself, then I got a funny feeling in my gut and decided to watch him through the window. I watched him nod at a car before three niggas jumped out with them big thangs.

180

Steady Mobbin'

For that split second, I made eye contact with all those niggas. Butta, Pressha and the lil' nigga, Pull-Out. It seemed like time went in slow motion as I watched Butta lift that AK in the air.

"Get down!" I yelled, then hit the deck right on time.

Yoppa! Yoppa! Yoppa! Yoppa! Yoppa! Boom! Boom! Boom! Boc! Boc! Boc!

Those niggas were trying to knock our heads off and didn't give a fuck who got killed in the process. I heard a man scream, then a body hit the ground right next to me. I looked at him laid out with that hole in his face. *Fuck that*, I told myself then pulled that Glock 30 from my hoody.

Yoppa! Yoppa! Yoppa! Yoppa! Yoppa!

That AK was going through the walls and out the back, destroying anything on contact. I heard chunks of the walls being ripped apart and falling to the floor.

"If we let these niggas get in here, it's a wrap!" I yelled out.

Boom! Boom! Boom! Boom! Boc! Boc! Yoppa! Yoppa! Yoppa! Yoppa!

I saw two more people fall that tried to run. I pumped myself up like always. *Take a deep breath, I know what I'm doing.*

I jumped up shooting as soon as I heard a pause.

Boom! Boom! Boom! Boom! Boom! Boom!

I let loose trying to' knock a head off. I must have surprised them, because they retreated a lil bit. That's when my niggas smelled blood in the water.

Boca! Boca! Boca! Boca! Boca! Bloc! Bloc! Bloc! Boom! Boom! Boom!

We got to eating those niggas up, it was car windows shattering everywhere. They were shooting while back peddling.

Boom! Boom! Boom! Boc! Boc! Boc! Boc!

We were bustin' right back, fuck it. I was thinking about rushing outside and taking the fight to the parking lot until that big bitch erased all of those thoughts.

Yoppa! Yoppa! Yoppa! Yoppa! Yoppa!

181

We all got back low not trying to take one of those 'k' shells.
"Gutta Squad!" One of them yelled.
"Caariippp!" The others followed.
They're showing out, I thought. That's when I started hearing sirens. "C'mon, we 'bout to shoot our way out the back," I said, then popped up, bustin'.
Boom! Boom! Boom! Boom! Boom! Boc! Boc! Boc! Boc! Bloc! Bloc! Bloc! Boom! Boom!
We got back on those niggas while walking backwards to the exit. Soon as I stepped outside, I started running around the building trying to get to my car before the police did. If those niggas were still standing there, then fuck it, we were all going to jail, 'cause I damn sho wasn't laying down.
By the time we got to the lot, they were long gone, so we jumped in our whips and sped out right before the boys got there. We literally drove right past they ass as they were speeding to the crime scene. I just know it was about five dead people inside that shop.
"I'ma kill those crab ass niggas!" I yelled, punching the steering wheel out of frustration.
"On my mama, blood, they got me fucked up," Bleed huffed.
I had that lil nigga's face saved in my brain. I was gone find that fuck boy and torture his ass. He really tried to set us up for the kill, I told myself. That's when I decided we were about to turn it up another level.
"You know that lil' nigga set us up right?" I asked five minutes later out of nowhere.
"I'ma kill that nigga, blood, on me," Bleed leaned his seat back.
It had already been a long day and it had just got started. The drama was far from over.

Hours Later

Me and Bleed ended up going to Blue Lake Park like originally planned. We planned to fall back on going, feeling like shit was gone be way too hot, but changed our minds after seeing the news. Nobody was killed at the barber shop, but one person was in critical condition. I figured it would be so many shootings that day, plus a couple of murders like every fourth of July, that our shit would be overshadowed.

Blue Lake was the perfect spot to have any family get together, especially on the Fourth, that came with the summer heat and fire crackers. That spot was so big, it could easily fit ten families and some extra.

I jumped out the 'Rati' rockin' a different outfit than the one I had on earlier, for obvious reasons. Now I had on some white linen shorts, a white tee and ice white Forces to go with it. I even left the vest in the car, which felt weird to me. I had gotten way too attached to it.

Everybody was at that park, all of us, with our women and children having a good time for the first time in what felt like forever. All the homies kept asking us what happened at the shop, but I kept slow playing them until it was safe to talk. Soon as the women started feeding the kids, I knew it was coming.

"Aight, blood, ain't no extra ears around now, what the fuck happened?" asked Burnside the moment the kids walked away.

Me and Bleed spent over ten minutes telling the same story from our points of view. Those niggas were into the story, asking hundreds of questions and shit like they ain't been in dozens of shootings themselves.

"How the fuck that nigga let off that 'K' and not kill shit? That bitch ass nigga wasn't tryna kill nobody," said Gotti.

"On God," Burnside added.

"Y'all ain't recognize the lil' nigga?" asked Gotti.

"Nope, and the whole time he was just sitting there with me laying the trap. He was already plotting on me but when they showed up, that made it even better," Bobbie finally spoke. He had been quiet the whole time, which is unlike him.

Fuck wrong with this nigga, I wondered.

"Yo' son, y'all niggas were slippin'. Y'all lucky to even be alive right now, word is bond. This the type of shit that happens when you play with niggas. They food, and we shoulda been ate," Jersey Joe said, irritating the fuck out of me. He had a thing about saying the wrong shit at the wrong time.

"Man, shut yo ass up! Since you know so much, show us where they live at, so we can go eat them niggas," Burnside flashed on him.

"This y'all city, nigga, y'all should have been did the homework. I'm just saying we need to hurry up and crush these niggas, son!" Joe shot back.

At that point, I just sat back down and listened to Joe argue with everybody for another five minutes. The shit was actually quite funny and very entertaining. Joe never knew when to shut up, that's just how he was, and he always spoke his mind, period.

Olay brought me a plate to eat. I sat there eating chicken while those dummies kept arguing. That's when I noticed Bobbie standing there muggin' Joe, not saying nothing.

"Bobbie, what's up, nigga? You usually the loudest in an argument," I asked, making everybody focus on him.

"I'm tired of this bitch ass nigga right here, blood," he said, staring Joe right in the eyes.

Aww shit, here we go.

Everybody got silent looking from Bobbie to Joe in confusion. I'm sure they could sense that his words were way deeper than the current conversation. I knew they were gone bump heads over that bitch eventually. I tried in vain to prevent it.

"What you say, bitch ass nigga?" Joe shot back, walking right up on him.

"You heard what I said, tender dick ass nigga! What's up with you speakin' on me to the bitch in those text messages, nigga!" Bobbie yelled in his face.

"Nigga, I ain't gotta speak on you to no bitch. I like to get up close and personal with mines, word is bond," Joe spat, his subliminal not going unnoticed.

184

Steady Mobbin'

They stood there, face to face, noses touching, staring each other down. Two killers, both predators, neither one willing to back down. I should have broken it up.

"Fuck yo word and yo bond, nigga, I got all the texts you sent to Falon, right here in my phone." Bobbie pulled his phone out.

Joe slapped the phone out of his hand before he even got the chance to scroll through the messages. That was the moment that did it, everything went downhill from there. Bobbie took the gun off his waist and passed it to Gotti.

"You gone need a gun if you plan on fuckin' with me, son," Joe taunted him.

Bobbie didn't say a word, he just took off on him. The first blow hit him dead in the mouth making him stumble back a few steps. Joe put his hand to his mouth, then looked at the blood that was on it. I would never forget the look on his face.

"I'ma kill you for that, son," he stated real calm, then rushed Bobbie throwing nothing but hay makers.

Joe had heart like a muthafucka, but fighting head up, wasn't his specialty. He kept putting his head down and swinging wild. Even though he was unorthodox, those muthafuckas were hot! He definitely had power behind each punch, but Bobbie had hands, so he was ducking his punches, while landing his own.

A small crowd had formed and was watching the fight. Olay came and stood next to me with our son. "Break them up, Marshawn!" she whispered, but I let them go on.

I felt like those niggas were grown ass men and needed to get that shit off their chests. We did end up having to break it up, after Bobbie slammed him and was sitting on his chest.

"Bitch ass nigga!" Bobbie yelled, while trying to break free from me and Bleed's grip.

"Square back up, bitch!" Joe yelled, breaking free from Burnside trying to rush back in.

Gotti grabbed him right before he could blindside Bobbie and Joe went crazy.

185

"Let me go, son! I'ma kill that bitch ass nigga! Word is bond!" he yelled, struggling to get free.

"Keep talkin that killer shit and we definitely gone get to it," Bobbie said real calm, then picked his phone up off the ground.

I looked at Falon and shook my head. *Dumb bitch.*

"Take that nigga to the car so he can cool off for a while," I told Burnside, I felt like if they kept sending threats, then somebody was gone start shooting.

Smack!

I turned my head in the direction of that unmistakable sound. Falon was sitting on the ground holding her face, looking stupid. Bobbie had slapped fire from her silly ass.

"Fuck wrong with you, bitch! I read yo texts, you and that nigga sitting around speaking on me, bitch. You playing both sides and that's a dangerous game. I'm done with yo' snake ass." He stood over her, yelling in her face.

Olay ran over and shoved the shit out of him. "What the fuck is wrong with you, hitting my sister like that?" she yelled, then pushed him again.

I snatched her ass up, then started yelling in her face. "Stop putting yo' hands on niggas! Fuck wrong with you, and now you wanna intervene? I been told you to talk to her ho ass, now niggas out here fighting!"

Falon hopped off the ground and pushed me like I was the one that slapped her. "Nigga, fuck you, you ain't shit either! You calling me a ho, but you the biggest one here! Why don't you tell my sister how your side bitch is pregnant! How she all on Facebook talkin' about it. Tell her how you spent every night at that bitch's house while she was gone, but I'm the ho? Nigga, you got some nerve," she blasted me with each word, and I felt the heat.

I was mad as a muthafucka, but there wasn't nothing I could say. I was busted. I looked at Olay and as we locked eyes, I knew she read my guilt, her pain was all over her face. So, I did the only thing I could do, only thing to say.

Steady Mobbin'

"That's gone cost you yo' life," I stared right through Falon, as I threatened her.

Her punk ass blew up my spot 'cause she got caught up. Didn't nobody tell her to do that snake shit, she had to know it would backfire. Now she putting my business out there breaking my bitch heart in the process. She didn't give me the chance to come clean, she took that from me.

I was heated!

"So, it's true, Marshawn?" Olay asked, sounding defeated.

I looked at her. She was ready to break down and that shit hurt my soul. "We'll talk about it at home. It's more to the story," I answered, coming off the wrong way.

Smack!

The next thing I knew, Olay had slapped the shit out of me and my glasses went flying through the air. It seemed like everybody was looking at me, waiting to see how I responded to that stunt. I felt my anger rising, I felt the demons in me coming alive. She knew better than to put her hands on me like that. Didn't wifey know I'd killed for much less?

My son started crying and when I looked down at him, my anger started fading away. Olay picked him up, then stared right at me. I could see the hurt and the anger now.

"I fuckin' hate you, nigga!" She said it so calmly chills ran down my spine.

"We'll see " I managed to say before walking away.

Bleed handed me my glasses and looked at me like, *What's next?* "Let's get the fuck outta here before I kill one of these bitches', blood," I said, then I started speed walking to the car.

"So, what's the move now?" Gotti asked, after we all made it to the parking lot.

"Fuck it, let's go get on one," Burnside suggested like always.

That was the perfect idea at the time, blow some steam off. Plus, I hadn't forgot about that shit that they did at the barber shop earlier that day. It was time to kill somebody. My soul was begging for a body.

"I'ma kill that lil nigga Pull-Out. I can't wait to catch his young ass. I wanted his big brother, now I want him more," Bobbie said, after turning the music down in the car.

We had been riding around for over an hour at the point. Me, him and Bleed were inside of one stolen car, while Burnside, Joe and Gotti was in the other. We knew our enemies were out somewhere, we just had to find them pussies.

"I'm definitely crushin' that nigga for that shit he did at the store on me," I agreed, thinking about how he had shot me, and how I would've been dead like Trell had I not been wearing a vest. My anger rose again.

"I'ma slide by the Playpen. I heard those niggas be up in there," Bobbie said.

The Playpen was one the most poppin' strip clubs in Portland and all type of niggas be up in there. It was on 60th and Columbia Street which wasn't in nobody's hood so there's no telling who was in there on any given night.

Dirty ass black hoody fina put it on/and you know exactly who we lookin' for/couldn't find 'em, so we finna look some mo.

Mozzy's lyrics were the only sounds in the car for the next ten minutes. It was something about his music that made us wanna kill.

"Aight, we here," Bobbie said, as he pulled into the parking lot.

He snapped me out of my zone, I had been thinking about the look of hurt in Olay's eyes. I couldn't stop thinking about her and how the whole situation unfolded. I was sick about it. I put my face to the window to see if I could spot any faces or cars that I knew.

"There go a group of niggas right there," Bleed said, pointing at a group of about twenty people.

"Pull up," I demanded, then tossed my Glock 30 on the seat and picked the AR-15 up off the floor.

Steady Mobbin'

Fuck that handgun. I planned on hitting those niggas with that big shit. Having 'em looking like a shark took a chunk out of 'em.

Click! Click!

Take a deep breath. I know what I'm doing.

"That's those Hoover niggas, you know today they hood day. They probably on gangsta time too," Bobbie informed me, as he parked right next to them.

I rolled the window down when I spotted a few of them that I fucked with. Once they spotted us, a few of them got to clutching but it would have been too late by then.

"Yo, Hooch, it's O-Dawg, what's brackin?" I called out, not concerned at all about them reaching for their weapons. They knew they were slippin' and if I was the enemy, they would've been in trouble.

"What's up with my nigga Groove?" he replied, walking up to the window all smiles.

"We out here tryna' purge, you know what it is," I answered, showing him the assault rifle.

He stuck his head in the car, looked at everybody then stepped back. "Yeah, I heard about that barber shop shit too. You know we don't fuck with those niggas either," he said, then nodded at Bobbie.

"Who in the club? We on those Piru niggas too," I asked.

"Nobody y'all want. We bout to hit a few more spots up, if I see those niggas, I'ma tap in," he promised.

"Please do, and I gotta bounty on those pussies too. Twenty bands for any top Piru, forty on Big Floyd." I threw that out there and watched the dollar signs flash in his eyes.

"That nigga said what, Groove?" a voice said out of the crowd, then he walked over.

It was another one I fucked with, Gatman.

"You heard me, nigga, and what's up with you? You weren't gone speak?"

"My bad, but what's up with that paper? You serious?" He sounded anxious.

Marcellus Allen

"Dead," I replied.

"If we see those Gutta niggas, I'll call you. If y'all see the sissies, then do the same." Hooch jumped back in.

They were always looking for the Rollin' 60's Crips, who they called 'the sissies' to diss their hood.

"Aight, blood, we gone." I tapped the seat so Bobbie would slide out.

We got up, with no specific destination in mind. That's how it was when we were head hunting. A whole bunch of driving around until we finally caught a nigga slippin'.

"You trust those niggas, blood?" Bleed asked.

"Not if we were in L.A., but I trust a few of them down here. Don't worry, we good," I answered, then went back to thinking about Olay.

I checked my phone to see if she had texted or called me. None. Fuck that bitch, I lied to myself. My phone started going off and for a split second, my heart got to beating fast thinking it was Olay, but it wasn't.

"What's mobbin'?" I answered for Burnside.

I listened to him for a few seconds and couldn't help but to crack a smile. What he told me was the best news I had heard all day. I hung up, still smiling.

"Drive by Sixtieth and Killingsworth, the homies got Ron, with his bitch ass." I couldn't stop cheesing if I wanted to. We had just got Pull-Out's best friend.

When we pulled up on 60th, the boys had the whole block tapped off. The car that Ron had been slumped in was still sitting at the intersection riddled with bullets. His bitch ass was still slumped on the steering wheel too. *Fuck that nigga*, I thought as we pulled into the gas station.

It was crowds of people everywhere. Police, news people, nosey people, snitches and his homies. We parked not even twenty feet away from his weak ass homies. I had my eyes locked on Butta and Pressha. I wanted to jump out so bad and torch all those niggas.

Steady Mobbin'

"There go Butta, Pressha, Gucci Ty, Half Dead and Pull-Out right there. I wanna bake those niggas," Bobbie spat, mirroring my thoughts.

"You think we can get away with it?" Bleed asked.

I had to battle with my pride and keep my emotions in check. I was staring at the nigga that killed Trell. The one who shot me and grazed my bitch in the head. I looked around at all the pigs, including the ho ass gang task.

"Naw, we wouldn't get far. We got one tonight, that's gone have to be enough," I said, then looked down at my gun in my hand. I gripped it tighter. "Pull up right on the side of them," I demanded.

"What's the move?" Bobbie asked, as he crept up on them.

"I'ma rub it in."

Bitch ass niggas, I thought as we got closer to the group of enemies. I rolled my window down and looked right in Butta's eyes. *Yeah, it's me.* I stared him down. He was in fight or flight mode, as he looked at the black instrument of death that was in my hands.

"Mob up or get shot down, y'all know what time it is. Fuck yo' dead homie, nigga, we did that. If you really mad, come around the corner then," I spat, while holding the AR-15 in the air, so they all could see it.

"You're a dead man," Butta shot back, but his eyes were telling a different story.

"Naw, the dead nigga is in that car over there with his brains missing," I hit him under the belt.

"Fuck slobs, nigga!" Pull-Out yelled, he was all in his emotions. Tears coming down his face and shit.

"Fuck *with* us," was my last words, then we drove off on those fuck boys.

I looked behind me and saw Pressha making gun motions at us with his hands. I had accomplished my mission and got to see firsthand how sick they were. Fuck those niggas.

Marcellus Allen

"Burnside said they caught him and his bitch coming out of his apartment and Gotti jumped out and roasted his ass," I filled them in on the details.

"His tender dick ass let the bitch live," Bobbie said, already knowing the truth.

Chapter 17
July 5th

Today was the day that we were having the sit down with Big Floyd at the request of Smoke. The meeting was being held at the used car dealership that Smoke owned. He told me to only bring one person with me and leave guns in the car. *Yeah, fuckin' right.* I told that nigga it's a deal, but I wanted Mike there. I wanted him to face me like a man.

"I hate these niggas, blood," I said to Bobbie, as I parked the 'Rati.'

I was mad about the situation with Olay, but I was willing to take it out on whoever. She still wasn't talking to me and wouldn't let me come home, so I stayed at Tamia's spot. I only got one text from her ass all night.

'If you try and come home, I'm going to Falon's with Mar Mar. I hate you.' That's what she said.

"All this shit over a bitch!" he replied, then cocked his gun back.

We jumped out at ten o'clock on the dot just like Smoke asked. He wanted the meeting to take place before the noon lunch hour when it was no customers. I also think he wanted us to feel safe in a business setting in broad daylight. *Yeah, right!* I tucked the Glock .40 in the small of my back. Fuck what he was talking about.

Smoke was waiting for us as soon as we stepped inside.

"What's brackin' y'all?" the O.G. Blood greeted us.

Smoke was about six feet five inches, two hundred fifty pounds, light skinned and wore his hair in two long braids. He was still stuck in the late nineties.

"We gucci, let's get this shit out the way," I replied, after we both shook him up.

He led us to the garage where Floyd and Mike were already waiting. The layout was perfect and real secluded. It was just an empty garage with a table and five chairs around it. The tension was thick in the air, but that was expected. Both of those niggas were standing up behind their side of the table sizing us up. I looked right in Mike's eyes and he looked away like the coward he was.

"Alright y'all, everybody take a seat and let's get to the bottom of this shit," Smoke announced, taking a seat.

Me and Bobbie sat down next, letting them win that small battle. Smoke stared at them until they sat down.

"Now, who wants to speak first?" he asked.

I looked at Bobbie and nodded, giving him the go to be the first one to break the silence. All that tough guy shit was killin' me anyways. They weren't built like that.

"I do," Bobbie said then cleared his throat.

Then with lightning speed, he jumped up and shot Mike dead in his face.

Boom! Boom!

Me and Floyd hopped up next, with Floyd reaching for his gun. I already had mine aimed at his head. We came prepared for this, they didn't.

"Go ahead and reach, nigga," I dared him, while smirking.

He moved his hand away from his waist and put them in the air in surrender.

"Tell your niece it wasn't personal."

Boom! Boom! Boom!

All chest shots. He stumbled backwards doing the shack then dropped to the ground. I stood over him like the predator that I was.

Boom! Boom!

I took his soul from him, then sat back down at the table. I laid the smoking gun on top of it, then looked at Smoke who never got out of his chair. He held eye contact while not showing the slightest sight of fear.

He's seen too many people die, I told myself.

"I thought you said no weapons, they both had guns," I ended the stare down.

"You just disrespected me by what you just did," he stated, too calm for me, totally ignoring what I had said.

194

"That makes us two disrespectful niggas then, cause I feel the same way," I replied.

"If I wanted to set you up, I would of took those guns at the door and let them keep theirs. You're too smart not to use your head, blood."

Good point. I wasn't really trippin' anyways. I was expecting for them niggas to have those guns on 'em. We played a dangerous game and won. I did feel some type of way about how he said we disrespected him. It wasn't necessarily what he said, but how he said it.

"Man, fuck those dead niggass, let's focus on the future now. They played with fire and got burned, fuck 'em. So, what's up, you feel some type of way or what?" I wanted to get down to the root of shit.

"You killed somebody in my place of business!" He raised his voice and slapped the table. "You've made my word not mean shit now! Of course, I feel some type of way, lil nigga." He stood up now.

I was doing everything in my power to stay calm at that point, but he was making it hard. *Don't react off emotions,* I warned myself. Bobbie gave me that look, he was getting fed up with the antics.

"Do you wanna talk like men, so we can fix the situation or do you wanna go to war? Cause it sound like that's what you want," I asked, trying hard not to space on his ass.

He looked at me like I had two heads and just said the dumbest shit in the world. "War? You lil niggas don't know what that means. Don't make me laugh. I can have half of Compton down here with one phone call, and I should too, since y'all like killin' Pirus anyways," he threatened and disrespected us.

Now I was mad. "I wouldn't give a fuck if you moved the whole city of Compton down here, nigga. My roots ain't from Compton, it's from 109th and Figueroa Street, and you know that. You might wanna cut the threats out." I stood up so we were eye to eye. "Piru don't run Portland, nigga, I do." I stuck my chest out there.

"I guess we'll see then." The tone of his voice let us know exactly what he meant by that.

Boom! Boom! Boom!

I had heard the shots then saw Smoke grab his chest before crumbling to the floor. I looked at Bobbie who was still sitting in his chair calm as fuck like he hadn't just smoked a made nigga. *It's war time now,* I thought as I walked over to Big Floyd. He was still alive, but barely breathing. He looked at me with defiance, then at Bobbie as he came over with his gun pointed at him.

"Pull that trigga and you'll be dead in days," Smoke threatened.

Boom! Boom! Boom! Boom!

"But you're dead now," said Bobbie, speaking to the corpse that he had just shot in the head multiple times.

I shook my head at him. "I hope you know what you just did, nigga." At that point, it didn't really matter, and I knew that.

"We were gone have to do it anyways. He was gone have us killed," he rationalized, then tucked his gun back on his waist.

I looked around at the carnage that we left laying around. Three bodies that were going to have to be answered for. Three Blood niggas dead on the floor of a car dealership. I rubbed my head sensing a headache coming. I knew what time it was.

"Nigga, you about to wash they feet and pray for 'em or what? You lookin' all nervous and shit," Bobbie taunted me.

This nigga always thinkin' shit a joke, I thought.

"Let's go grab the surveillance tapes and get the fuck outta here, blood," I said, then left his ass standing there.

Pull that trigga and you'll be dead in days. I couldn't get those words out my head as I made my way into the office. I had a bad feeling for some reason in the pit of my gut that I couldn't shake. I knew shit was going to hit the fan, but not like it did. I should have listened to my gut. I should have fuckin' listened.

Steady Mobbin'

July 8th

It was a Saturday night and I decided to stay in with Tamia. Olay was still on her *Diary of A Mad Black Woman* trip, so going to my house wasn't a option. Tamia couldn't have been happier with the arrangement. Especially since I had been in the house since we killed those three niggas.

The town was on fire and niggas were getting burnt left and right the past couple of days. I had stayed in the house while everybody was out there fuckin' the city up. Every time I turned the news on, they were reporting another shooting. I got tired of seeing the bitch ass gang task sending threats and making promises they knew they couldn't keep.

Those Murda Squad niggas were definitely trying to purge something. Nobody knew exactly who killed Floyd, Mike and Smoke at the dealership, but we were on the top of everybody's list. We had random niggas shootin' up our blocks at all times of the day. I was waiting for shit to calm down, then I was going in beast mode for the disrespect.

"It feel good, daddy?" Tamia asked, sitting on my lower back, giving me a massage.

I was laying facing the bottom of the bed watching my favorite movie *Shottas*. "Hell yeah, that shit feel good, baby," I moaned out. Her fingers were hitting all the right spots.

My phone started going off, but I was feeling too relaxed to reach for it. "Keep doing that, baby," I told Tamia, after I felt her pouring some more of that oil on me and rubbing it in.

My phone went off another three times, before I finally gave in and had Tamia hand it to me. I seen it was Gotti calling and I put it on speakerphone, then laid back down.

"Blood, you fuckin up my date night, what you want?" I answered, not feeling like dealing with no petty shit or the latest gossip.

He exhaled real slow, then tried to speak, but couldn't get the words fully out. He was crying, but trying to hold it in. My heart dropped. I knew it was bad.

"They got, they got..."

"They got what? What happened, nigga?" I yelled, jumping up and knocking Tamia to the floor. *Maybe it's about some money,* I tried to lie to myself.

"Bobbie's dead. They killed my nigga," he finally managed to get it out.

It felt like my heart had been ripped out of my chest. I'd never felt pain so deep. I ran my hand over my face, then exhaled.

"Where's he at? What happened and who did it?" I asked, feeling the evil in me creep out.

"They caught him in his car on 15th and Prescott on the side of the store. We clacked it out with those Gutta Squad niggas downtown, but we all got away. Next thing we know, he dead ten minutes later over there," he explained, still trying to hide his tears but I could hear it in his voice.

"Everybody meet at the dungeon," I said, then hung up.

I'm killin' half the city! I vowed to myself. I looked at Tamia, who was standing there covering her mouth with her hand, crying. That's when I broke down crying with her. I couldn't stop the tears from falling down my face even though I tried to. Tamia wrapped her arms around me tightly, crying in my chest. She loved Bobbie too.

I forced myself to pull it together and get in beast mode. I broke away from her, got dressed and grabbed my gun without speaking a word. My phone kept ringing, so I turned it off, there wasn't nothing to say. My best friend was dead.

Tamia watched in silence, she knew better than to try to stop me. When I got to the front door, she ran and hugged me, then kissed my lips before telling me to be safe.

Time to purge.

Steady Mobbin'

I pulled up to the crime scene twenty minutes later, parking across the street. I seen my nigga's red Monte Carlo sitting in the lot surrounded by pigs taking pictures and all that other CSI shit. The vultures and nosey muthafuckas were out there too. Couldn't wait to gossip. *Just wait, I'ma give y'all summin' to talk about,* I thought, as I jumped from the car.

It was all eyes on me as I crossed the street, but I had tunnel vision. I ignored everybody that called my name or tried to wave me down. I wanted to see exactly how they had did my nigga. I was denied the privilege as soon as my feet touched that side of the street by none other than the house niggas.

"Come on, Marshawn, you know we can't let you pass the tape. You don't wanna see him like that, trust me." Detective Rogers blocked me from walking on their crime scene.

"Tell me what happened, then," I growled.

"You know we can't discuss the investigation with you, either. I'm sorry, but anything you could tell us will help us solve this case faster." He had the nerve to come at a real nigga in that sucka shit.

I stared down both of those punks, then tried my luck with Detective Freeman. "If I don't start getting some answers, I'ma have y'all rushing to three new crime scenes by the time the sun rises and that's on my son's heartbeat," I threatened.

They looked at each other confused on what to do. They knew I was dead serious. They could hear it in my voice and see it in my eyes. They knew I had the power to make it happen and they didn't want that. I looked around them to the scene. I noticed something that stood out to me.

"Just answer this one question for me and I'll be content with that," I tried to reason.

"And what's that?" Detective Rogers took the bait.

"I don't see no marker cards on the ground or no bullet casings. Why is that?" I asked.

They looked at each other again, then Rogers spoke up. "The shooter got up close. Either he put the gun all the way in the car or he was sitting in the car. Two shots to the head. Both casings are in the car," he explained to me. *What the fuck? Why would he let an enemy get that close? Who was he talkin' to if that was the case?* Those were my thoughts, as I headed back to my car. I left with more questions than I came with. I was hoping that my niggas could shed some light on the situation. Whoever did it, knew exactly what they were doing. It didn't matter, cause I was killin' everybody that wasn't on my side.

Next Day

I woke up the next morning with a horrible feeling in my gut. It was like my heart had a hole in it. *Please Lord, let it all have been a dream,* I prayed as I unwrapped myself from Tamia, getting out the bed. The tears that escaped my eyes voluntarily mixed with the evil I felt circulating through my veins, confirming that shit was real.

"Are you okay, baby?" Tamia sat up in the bed. Her eyes were red and puffy from crying all night.

Am I okay? I'll never be okay, I told myself.

"Naw, I'm not. Stop stressing yourself before you harm the baby," I mumbled.

"Are you hungry?"

"I'm good," I answered, then made my way to the couch in the front room.

I stared at the half ounce of cocaine that I had left on the table. That's when flashes of last night started flooding my mind. After I left the scene, I met up with everybody at our war room that we called 'the dungeon'! One by one, they all explained how they had ran straight into the Gutta niggas downtown and everybody started shooting on sight.

Nobody got shot from our side. Everybody ran to their cars and got the fuck up out of there. That's where their knowledge stopped. It was so many rumors circulating on who killed Bobbie, that the shit was way out of hand.

200

Muthafuckas were even saying that gang task did it since they knew he had so many bodies but couldn't indict him. *Yeah fuckin' right.* I hit a fat line of powder.

That shit went straight to my head as I leaned back and held my head high in the air. *Pull that trigga and you'll be dead in days.* Smoke's threat played in my head. That was the main rumor I believed, those niggas got him. *Either one of those Murda Squad Piru's or one of those California niggas did it. I'm killin' all those niggas!* I told my inner demons then snorted another line. Sniff!

"Argghh!" I yelled at the top of my lungs, then jumped off the couch. "On my mama, I'm on niggas blood! Every day, blood! I'm purging niggas!" I screamed out, slamming my fist into my palm.

Tears were pouring from my eyes and I made no attempt to wipe them. I was getting ready to kill some shit. Tamia was standing in the hallway not knowing what to do. I walked right past her ass straight for the bedroom. I put my vest on, cause the cocaine had me feeling real paranoid. Then I called Burnside.

"Get everybody together right now, we on one. We going to purge in broad daylight and everything. We shuttin' the whole city down, fuck everybody," I said, hanging up on him before he could say a word.

I threw on an all-black Nike jump suit, grabbed my Glock 17, and headed for the door, high as a giraffe.

"Please be careful and come back home," Tamia pleaded with me.

I nodded, then walked out. I didn't plan on doing too much talkin' while I was in beast mode.

I stepped off the elevator with a mug on my face as I walked in the parking garage. It was dead silent but that was expected at nine o'clock in the morning. I heard a car door open as I was walking to the 'Rati' and looked in that direction out of pure paranoia. Tamia lived in a gated community, but when I saw a light skinned nigga with long hair walking towards me, my heart dropped. Gucci Ty.

"Yo' own kind wants you dead, cuz!" he yelled, then lifted his gun up.

I pulled mine from the hoody but was a lil late.

Boom! Boom! Boom! Boom! Boom! Bloc! Bloc! Bloc! Bloc!

We were both firing then I dropped to one knee. His bitch ass hit me in the leg, but I kept yanking from the ground.

Bloc! Bloc! Bloc! Bloc!

He stumbled back, giving me time to pull myself up and limp toward him, letting off shot after shot, while he did the same.

Boom! Boom! Bloc! Bloc! Bloc! Bloc! Boom! Boom! Bloc! Bloc!

We were walking towards each other, while shooting. I didn't know if he had hit me some more or if I had hit him at all. I didn't give a fuck! The cocaine had me feeling like Superman, plus I had the vest on. Then I saw his body start to twist and turn from the bullets I was tagging his ass with, but he kept shooting.

Boom! Boom! Boom! Boom! Bloc! Bloc! Bloc! Bloc! Bloc!

I watched him fall in slow motion it seemed like, then right when I told myself to finish him, that's when I fell and blacked out.

I woke up in a hospital bed a few days later not know what the fuck happened. As soon as I opened my eyes, my mother was standing over me raining kisses all over me and praising the Lord. I tried to talk, but my mouth was extremely dry. She brought over a glass of water with a straw for me to sip out of. That's when I noticed the long ass tubes that were in my nose going to my stomach to feed me. When the fuck they do that? I wondered to myself.

I sipped the water, as the shootout started playing in my mind. I *torched that nigga!*

"How many times did I get hit?" I asked, my voice sounding raspy as shit.

"Hold on, baby, let me get the doctor," Mama said then turned away.

I tried to lift my hand to stop her, but it was handcuffed to the bed. *What the fuck?*

"Mom?" I tried to raise my voice, but it was barely louder than a whisper.

"Yeah?" she asked.

"Is Olay or Tamia out there?" I asked not knowing what to expect.

"You don't know the half. They got kicked out yesterday and so did everybody else. I'll be right back," she said then disappeared out the door.

The doctor came in shortly after that with the house niggas right behind him. Aww shit, I thought to myself.

"Hello, Mr. Anderson, I'm Doctor Lewis. Can you hear me good?" he asked.

I nodded my head.

"You've been in and out of consciousness for the past four days and you're lucky to be alive. You were shot a total of three times, Mr. Anderson. Twice in your upper chest and one grazed the side of your head. Another six or seven bullets were stopped by the bulletproof vest you were wearing. Any questions?" he informed me.

"When can I get these tubes taken out?" That's all I wanted to know.

"We'll get them out sometime today."

"Also, since I'm heavily sedated and not in my right mind, I would like for those detectives to be taken out of here. I don't want them questioning me while I'm drugged."

I knew the type of games they liked to play when niggas were sedated. Fuck that, they weren't about to have me explaining my statements to the homies. I knew way too many niggas that be blaming their snitchin' on the medication.

"Listen, Marshawn, we're here to read you your rights and that's it. If you wanna talk after that, then that's on you," Detective Rogers jumped in.

203

Marcellus Allen

I stared at him like he was stupid for even talking to me. Fuck the police. "Marshawn Anderson, you're under arrest for the murder of Tyrone Johnson." I blocked out the rest of the bullshit he was spittin'. I already knew the drill. When he got done, he asked did I have any questions.

"When did he die?" I asked.

"Yesterday," he answered.

"I'm tired and I need my rest. So, get the fuck out and don't come back until it's time to take me downtown. Fuck the police, on the Mob." I rolled over and closed my eyes.

I couldn't believe I was going to jail for a body. I was sick, but I knew I had some beasts on retainer, so I would be gucci. This jail shit was a part of the game and to be expected. I couldn't cry about it, cause I signed up for it. Wasn't no snitchin' in me at all, not a drop. *I'ma stay Steady Mobbin', fuck the police,* I told myself.

I faintly heard one of the detectives snicker, as if he was reading my thoughts and was certain that I was going down for life.

Maybe so, but don't count on it.

That was the last thought I had before slipping back into unconsciousness.

To Be Continued...
Steady Mobbin' 2
Coming Soon

Submission Guideline.

Submit the first three chapters of your completed manuscript to ldpsubmissions@gmail.com, subject line: Your book's title. The manuscript must be in a .doc file and sent as an attachment. Document should be in Times New Roman, double spaced and in size 12 font. Also, provide your synopsis and full contact information. If sending multiple submissions, they must each be in a separate email.

Have a story but no way to send it electronically? You can still submit to LDP/Ca$h Presents. Send in the first three chapters, written or typed, of your completed manuscript to:

LDP: Submissions Dept
Po Box 870494
Mesquite, Tx 75187

DO NOT send original manuscript. Must be a duplicate.

Provide your synopsis and a cover letter containing your full contact information.

Thanks for considering LDP and Ca$h Presents.

Marcellus Allen

BOW DOWN TO MY GANGSTA

By **Ca$h**

TORN BETWEEN TWO

By **Coffee**

BLOOD STAINS OF A SHOTTA **III**

By **Jamaica**

STEADY MOBBIN

By **Marcellus Allen**

BLOOD OF A BOSS **V**

By **Askari**

LOYAL TO THE GAME **IV**

By **T.J. & Jelissa**

A DOPEBOY'S PRAYER **II**

By **Eddie "Wolf" Lee**

IF LOVING YOU IS WRONG... **III**

LOVE ME EVEN WHEN IT HURTS

By **Jelissa**

TRUE SAVAGE **V**

By **Chris Green**

TRAPHOUSE KING **III**

By **Hood Rich**

BLAST FOR ME **III**

By **Ghost**

ADDICTIED TO THE DRAMA **III**

By **Jamila Mathis**

LIPSTICK KILLAH **III**

CRIME OF PASSION **II**

By **Mimi**

Steady Mobbin'

WHAT BAD BITCHES DO **III**

By **Aryanna**

THE COST OF LOYALTY **II**

By **Kweli**

SHE FELL IN LOVE WITH A REAL ONE **II**

By **Tamara Butler**

LOVE SHOULDN'T HURT **II**

By **Meesha**

CORRUPTED BY A GANGSTA **III**

By **Destiny Skai**

A GANGSTER'S CODE II

By **J-Blunt**

KING OF NEW YORK II

By **T.J. Edwards**

CUM FOR ME **IV**

By **Ca$h & Company**

STEADY MOBBN' 2

By **Marcellus Allen**

Available Now

RESTRAINING ORDER **I & II**

By **CA$H & Coffee**

LOVE KNOWS NO BOUNDARIES **I II & III**

By **Coffee**

RAISED AS A GOON I, II, III & IV

BRED BY THE SLUMS I, II, III

BLAST FOR ME I & II

By **Ghost**

LAY IT DOWN **I & II**

207

Marcellus Allen

LAST OF A DYING BREED
BLOOD STAINS OF A SHOTTA I & II
By **Jamaica**
LOYAL TO THE GAME
LOYAL TO THE GAME II
LOYAL TO THE GAME III
By **TJ & Jelissa**
BLOODY COMMAS I & II
SKI MASK CARTEL I II & III
KING OF NEW YORK
By **T.J. Edwards**
IF LOVING HIM IS WRONG...I & II
By **Jelissa**
WHEN THE STREETS CLAP BACK I & II III
By **Jibril Williams**
A DISTINGUISHED THUG STOLE MY HEART I II & III
LOVE SHOULDN'T HURT
By **Meesha**
A GANGSTER'S CODE
By J-Blunt
PUSH IT TO THE LIMIT
By **Bre' Hayes**
BLOOD OF A BOSS **I, II, III & IV**
By **Askari**
THE STREETS BLEED MURDER **I, II & III**
THE HEART OF A GANGSTA I II& III
By **Jerry Jackson**
CUM FOR ME
CUM FOR ME 2
CUM FOR ME 3

Steady Mobbin'

An **LDP Erotica Collaboration**
BRIDE OF A HUSTLA **I II & II**
THE FETTI GIRLS **I, II& III**
CORRUPTED BY A GANGSTA I & II
By **Destiny Skai**
WHEN A GOOD GIRL GOES BAD
By **Adrienne**
A GANGSTER'S REVENGE **I II III & IV**
THE BOSS MAN'S DAUGHTERS
THE BOSS MAN'S DAUGHTERS II
THE BOSSMAN'S DAUGHTERS III
THE BOSSMAN'S DAUGHTERS IV
THE BOSS MAN'S DAUGHTERS **V**
A SAVAGE LOVE **I & II**
BAE BELONGS TO ME
A HUSTLER'S DECEIT I, II
WHAT BAD BITCHES DO I, II
By **Aryanna**
A KINGPIN'S AMBITON
A KINGPIN'S AMBITION **II**
I MURDER FOR THE DOUGH
By **Ambitious**
TRUE SAVAGE
TRUE SAVAGE II
TRUE SAVAGE **III**
TRUE SAVAGE **IV**
By **Chris Green**
A DOPEBOY'S PRAYER
By **Eddie "Wolf" Lee**
THE KING CARTEL **I, II & III**

209

Marcellus Allen

By **Frank Gresham**
THESE NIGGAS AIN'T LOYAL **I, II & III**
By **Nikki Tee**
GANGSTA SHYT **I II &III**
By **CATO**
THE ULTIMATE BETRAYAL
By **Phoenix**
BOSS'N UP **I , II & III**
By **Royal Nicole**
I LOVE YOU TO DEATH
By Destiny J
I RIDE FOR MY HITTA
I STILL RIDE FOR MY HITTA
By **Misty Holt**
LOVE & CHASIN' PAPER
By **Qay Crockett**
TO DIE IN VAIN
By **ASAD**
BROOKLYN HUSTLAZ
By **Boogsy Morina**
BROOKLYN ON LOCK I & II
By **Sonovia**
GANGSTA CITY
By **Teddy Duke**
A DRUG KING AND HIS DIAMOND I & II
A DOPEMAN'S RICHES
By Nicole Goosby
TRAPHOUSE KING I & II
By **Hood Rich**
LIPSTICK KILLAH **I, II**

Steady Mobbin'

CRIME OF PASSION
By **Mimi**
STEADY MOBBN'
By **Marcellus Allen**

Marcellus Allen

BOOKS BY LDP'S CEO, CA$H

TRUST IN NO MAN

TRUST IN NO MAN 2

TRUST IN NO MAN 3

BONDED BY BLOOD

SHORTY GOT A THUG

THUGS CRY

THUGS CRY 2

THUGS CRY 3

TRUST NO BITCH

TRUST NO BITCH 2

TRUST NO BITCH 3

TIL MY CASKET DROPS

RESTRAINING ORDER

RESTRAINING ORDER 2

IN LOVE WITH A CONVICT

Coming Soon

BONDED BY BLOOD 2

BOW DOWN TO MY GANGSTA

Steady Mobbin'